𝓍 𝔴 𝒶
1/31/11

Double-barreled Justice . . .

Longarm raised the cumbersome shotgun, cocked back its twin hammers, and slowly squeezed one of the triggers.

The blast was incredible! Longarm saw flames shoot out of one barrel, and the recoil punched him so hard he staggered. Taking aim again, he fired off the second barrel with similar thundering effect. Barrels smoking, Longarm reloaded the awesome weapon and raced toward the camp. When he saw Horn's gunmen jumping up from their blankets, he opened fire again with both barrels blazing.

An outlaw was swept off the ground and hurled backward as if a giant and invisible hand had plucked him into the sky. Longarm dropped the shotgun, dove behind some brush, and pulled his six-gun as the slave women opened fire.

Gunsmoke and chaos reigned supreme and the outlaws that had not been killed in the opening salvo scattered like desert quail, taking their own firing positions.

D0837808

DON'T MISS THESE
ALL-ACTION WESTERN SERIES
FROM THE BERKLEY PUBLISHING GROUP

THE GUNSMITH by J. R. Roberts
Clint Adams was a legend among lawmen, outlaws, and ladies. They called him . . . the Gunsmith.

LONGARM by Tabor Evans
The popular long-running series about Deputy U.S. Marshal Custis Long—his life, his loves, his fight for justice.

SLOCUM by Jake Logan
Today's longest-running action Western. John Slocum rides a deadly trail of hot blood and cold steel.

BUSHWHACKERS by B. J. Lanagan
An action-packed series by the creators of Longarm! The rousing adventures of the most brutal gang of cutthroats ever assembled—Quantrill's Raiders.

DIAMONDBACK by Guy Brewer
Dex Yancey is Diamondback, a Southern gentleman turned con man when his brother cheats him out of the family fortune. Ladies love him. Gamblers hate him. But nobody pulls one over on Dex . . .

WILDGUN by Jack Hanson
The blazing adventures of mountain man Will Barlow—from the creators of Longarm!

TEXAS TRACKER by Tom Calhoun
J.T. Law: the most relentless—and dangerous—manhunter in all Texas. Where sheriffs and posses fail, he's the best man to bring in the most vicious outlaws—for a price.

→ TABOR EVANS ←

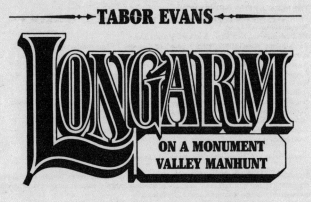

LONGARM

ON A MONUMENT VALLEY MANHUNT

JOVE BOOKS, NEW YORK

THE BERKLEY PUBLISHING GROUP
Published by the Penguin Group
Penguin Group (USA) Inc.
375 Hudson Street, New York, New York 10014, USA

Penguin Group (Canada), 90 Eglinton Avenue East, Suite 700, Toronto, Ontario M4P 2Y3, Canada
(a division of Pearson Penguin Canada Inc.)
Penguin Books Ltd., 80 Strand, London WC2R 0RL, England
Penguin Group Ireland, 25 St. Stephen's Green, Dublin 2, Ireland (a division of Penguin Books Ltd.)
Penguin Group (Australia), 250 Camberwell Road, Camberwell, Victoria 3124, Australia
(a division of Pearson Australia Group Pty. Ltd.)
Penguin Books India Pvt. Ltd., 11 Community Centre, Panchsheel Park, New Delhi—110 017, India
Penguin Group (NZ), 67 Apollo Drive, Rosedale, North Shore 0632, New Zealand
(a division of Pearson New Zealand Ltd.)
Penguin Books (South Africa) (Pty.) Ltd., 24 Sturdee Avenue, Rosebank, Johannesburg 2196,
South Africa

Penguin Books Ltd., Registered Offices: 80 Strand, London WC2R 0RL, England

This is a work of fiction. Names, characters, places, and incidents either are the product of the author's imagination or are used fictitiously, and any resemblance to actual persons, living or dead, business establishments, events, or locales is entirely coincidental.

LONGARM ON A MONUMENT VALLEY MANHUNT

A Jove Book / published by arrangement with the author

PRINTING HISTORY
Jove edition / September 2010

Copyright © 2010 by Penguin Group (USA) Inc.
Cover illustration by Miro Sinovcic.

All rights reserved.
No part of this book may be reproduced, scanned, or distributed in any printed or electronic form without permission. Please do not participate in or encourage piracy of copyrighted materials in violation of the author's rights. Purchase only authorized editions.
For information, address: The Berkley Publishing Group,
a division of Penguin Group (USA) Inc.,
375 Hudson Street, New York, New York 10014.

ISBN: 978-0-515-14837-4

JOVE®
Jove Books are published by The Berkley Publishing Group,
a division of Penguin Group (USA) Inc.,
375 Hudson Street, New York, New York 10014.
JOVE® is a registered trademark of Penguin Group (USA) Inc.
The "J" design is a trademark of Penguin Group (USA) Inc.

PRINTED IN THE UNITED STATES OF AMERICA

10 9 8 7 6 5 4 3 2 1

If you purchased this book without a cover, you should be aware that this book is stolen property. It was reported as "unsold and destroyed" to the publisher, and neither the author nor the publisher has received any payment for this "stripped book."

Chapter 1

United States Deputy Marshal Custis Long was sitting at his office desk at the Federal Building feeling bored, restless and uncharacteristically irritable. Nothing in the world put him out of sorts more than doing government paperwork. And even as he leaned back in his desk chair and clasped his hands behind his neck to stare up at the ceiling, Longarm knew that he had at least four hours' worth of paperwork facing him before quitting time at five o'clock this Friday.

"You're never going to get it done just sitting there gazing up at the darned ceiling," his boss, Billy Vail said. "So you might just as well sit up and get after it."

"I was hopin' you might volunteer to do the pencil work."

Billy shook his head. "Custis, you know that about eighty percent of my job is handling paperwork. So why on earth do you think that I'd be willing to do yours?"

"Just hopin', I guess." Longarm lifted his feet off his desk and sat up straight. "What if I told you that I was feelin' kinda puny this afternoon and thinkin' that I ought to go home and rest up for next Monday?"

"I'd say that you were trying to get out of doin' that paperwork. And I'd remind you that it's been sittin' on your desk for over two weeks. Now, come on, Custis! Just quit stallin' and jump right into those reports."

Longarm scowled and took his time selecting a pencil. He then got out his pen knife and carefully sharpened the pencil's point until it was about perfect. "Billy," Longarm said, not even looking up at his boss, "I don't know how you stand to sit at a desk so many hours a day and do these stupid government reports. I surely don't."

"I do the reports and fill out the forms because they're part of my job requirement. And if I don't get them finished on time and sent off to my bosses in Washington, D.C., then I'll get nasty letters and even urgent-sounding telegrams telling me to complete the paperwork . . . or start thinking about a new job."

"I haven't been out on a field assignment in over three weeks," Longarm said, not really listening to his boss. "Three weeks! Some kind of lawman I am. Why, I might as well be wearin' a nightshade and spectacles for all the lawman's work I've been doin' lately."

Billy sighed. "Custis, I send you out on more assignments than any other marshal in my office. And I always send you out for the most dangerous and difficult jobs . . . the ones that you prefer. So what if now and then things are a little quiet around here?"

"'Quiet' is a *real* understatement, Boss. This place has been like a morgue lately."

Billy shook his head. "Most folks are sort of grateful when the world outside hits a patch of peacefulness. They're actually glad when nobody gets mugged, murdered or beaten. But you're different, Custis. You thrive on chaos and bloodshed."

"I wouldn't exactly put it like that," Longarm protested. "I just like *action*. I like to be doin' somethin' important instead of messin' with these damned forms and reports."

Billy took a chair at an empty desk and studied his big deputy marshal. "All right," he said finally. "I was going to send Marshal Joe Timmons out on this one because he's from the Arizona Territory and he knows a thing or two about the Navajo . . . But since you're so unhappy, maybe I'll send you on the assignment instead . . . provided you finish up your paperwork and have it on my desk today by quittin' time."

"What is goin' on in the Arizona Territory?" Longarm said, suddenly all ears.

"Do you remember Marshal Fergus Horn?"

"How could anyone forget him?" Longarm asked. "He got fired about three years ago, didn't he?"

"Horn resigned under some pressure. We acknowledged that he had done some fine work for us, but that it was a mutual decision that Marshal Horn resign and hand over his badge."

"He was a big fella and he had a quick temper," Longarm said. "Worked out of the office in Santa Fe and was transferred here but didn't last but a month or two."

"That's right," Billy said. "Did you know that his young wife, Veronica, was former Colorado governor Charles Sutton's only daughter?"

"No," Longarm admitted. "But I saw her a time or two, and she was sure easy on the eyes."

"Yes," Billy agreed. "Veronica Horn was a stunning young woman, and no one that I ever talked to could understand why on earth she had seen fit to marry Fergus."

"As I recall," Longarm mused, "Fergus was a handsome fellow. Had this big smile and easy way around strangers. Said he was . . . that's right . . . said he was part Navajo."

"And he probably is."

Billy folded his hands in his lap. His hands were no longer strong and calloused as they'd once been, when he'd worked many different manual jobs as a young man trying to support his growing family. "Marshal Fergus Horn was hired by this department because he is part Indian and he told us that he could speak in several tongues. Ute. Apache and, of course, Navajo. We thought that the man would prove very useful, and he should have, except that he was a law unto himself. Horn ignored the rules of law and of this office. He operated as if *he* were the law and he didn't hesitate to be judge and executioner if he thought that the accused deserved a quick bullet or a knife in the heart."

"That happens to some lawmen," Custis said. "You sleep with dogs and you get fleas. You get around some of the worst of men and you just want to kill them, knowin' that you'll be doin' society one helluva big favor."

"Well," Billy said, "as you know, carrying a badge means that you have to enforce the laws and do your best to make sure that the guilty stand before a court of law and receive legal justice. But Horn just never saw things that way. He figured that he was saving taxpayers time and money if he just settled the matter as he saw fit to settle it."

"So what happened to him and why are we talkin' about the man three years after he left office?" Longarm asked.

"After he was fired from this office, Fergus Horn's wife left him . . . but he never accepted the fact and he fought the divorce. Since Veronica was the daughter of a powerful and influential man, Horn had no hope of keeping his wife . . . and I seriously doubt that he ever deserved her. But when Horn was served papers stating that the divorce was finalized, he vowed to take matters into his own hands and take back his wife by force, if necessary."

"In what way?"

"He vowed to kill the judge that signed the divorce decree. And he also vowed to kill former governor Charles Sutton. And guess what?"

Longarm's blue gray eyes narrowed. "Are they *both* dead?"

"They are. Everyone knows that former governor Sutton was thrown from his horse out east of Denver and his neck was broken. But few know or remember that the judge who signed the Horn divorce decree was found only a day later, dead in his home with a fish bone lodged down deep in his throat."

"It happens."

"Sure," Billy said, "but one day apart? And no wit-

nesses in either case? Charles Sutton was well known as
an expert horseman. What are the odds that he would be
riding alone and land on his neck?"

Longarm shrugged. He didn't know where this conversation was headed, but it sure was more interesting
than the stack of paperwork on his desk.

"And here's something else that I'm sure will pique
your interest," Billy said. "Everyone who knew the judge
was aware that the man hated fish. Couldn't stand the sight,
smell or the taste of it."

"Huh."

"So we have the deaths of the two men that Fergus
Horn swore to kill occur in the space of two days . . .
both unwitnessed."

"Did the local sheriff and his men investigate? See
any sign of foul play or even footprints or horse prints
around the governor, or any signs of a forced entry at the
judge's house?"

"They found nothing that would suggest murder . . .
but people who knew about Horn's threats have no doubt
that he carried them out."

The governor died . . . what? Two years ago?"

"Give or take a few weeks."

"And Horn was forced to resign from this office almost three years ago?"

"That's right," Billy said. "But here's where it gets
even more interestin'. Fergus vanished at the same time
his wife disappeared. Fergus always swore that he knew
where to find buried Spanish gold and silver in Arizona.
A fortune's worth."

"What do you suppose really happened to his wife,
Veronica?"

Billy reached into his vest pocket and withdrew a letter that was stained by what appeared to be red dirt. "This was sent to our current governor. It's a note, supposedly from Veronica, saying that she is being held hostage in the Arizona Territory by her former husband. The tone of the note is one of desperation, and the woman claims that her ex-husband is inciting the Navajo to go on the warpath."

"The 'warpath'?" Longarm asked with surprise.

"That's right. As I'm sure you remember, during the winter of eighteen sixty-three to sixty-four, about eight thousand of 'em were defeated by Colonel Kit Carson and sent off on what they call the Long Walk to some godforsaken place in New Mexico. It's my understanding that there are three hundred miles of hell between Fort Defiance, Arizona, and Fort Sumner in New Mexico."

"Yeah, I recall readin' about that when I was fightin' in the War Between the States," Longarm said. "A lot of Indians died on that forced march. And I seem to recall that the Army, in all its wisdom, put them on a reservation where their Apache enemies were already settled. I imagine that a lot of the Navajo either froze to death or starved before they were allowed to return to their own land a few years later."

"That's right," Billy said. "The relocation of the Navajo to New Mexico has been acknowledged as a complete federal disaster. The Navajo have traditionally been shepherds. What the army tried to make them farmers in New Mexico, the Navajo failed in large part due to lack of irrigation and poor soil. After a huge death toll at Fort Sumner, the Navajo were finally allowed to return to their reservation. So you can imagine that white people are not very welcome on the Navajo Reservation today. In fact, the Navajo have made it clear that any white invaders coming onto their land to mine or graze livestock are going to be attacked and killed."

"But Fergus Horn, bein' part Navajo, would have a free pass."

"Correct," Billy said. "But his wife . . . or I should say ex-wife . . . bein' white, would be in great danger."

"Did the letter come with a postmarked envelope?"

"Nobody knows how it was sent, or from where, or even if it is authentic. But Veronica hasn't been seen since shortly after the funeral of her father."

"The letter might be a hoax," Longarm said.

"For what purpose?"

"For the purpose of drawin' out a United States Marshal to that huge reservation and then killin' him," Longarm replied.

"But why would Fergus Horn want that to happen?"

"I have no earthly idea," Longarm answered. "But let's say that he did want to start a Navajo uprisin'. Maybe even another Long Walk to some distant shit-hole like Fort Sumner. That would pretty much empty out Navajo lands of its people, wouldn't it?"

"Yes, I guess it would."

"And let's say that Horn found a gold or silver mine on the reservation."

"I see where you are goin' with this," Billy Vail said, nodding. "But we don't even know if Fergus Horn is still alive, much less if this letter purported to be written by his former wife is legitimate."

"Only one way to find that out," Longarm said, grinning.

Billy chuckled. "You finish up those reports and that paperwork and come Monday morning. I'll . . ."

"If the woman's life is in danger and Fergus is plottin' a full-scale Navajo uprisin', can we really afford to have me sit around fillin' out forms? I'd think that you'd want me on the next westbound train out of Denver, which as you well know leaves . . ."

Longarm consulted his gold pocket watch, which had a derringer cleverly attached to the watch fob and chain. "It leaves in about two hours. Just enough time for me to get to my apartment, pack a bag and reach the train station to buy a first-class ticket on the government's dime."

"First class?"

"I might be able to prevent an entire Indian war, Billy! And to do that, I'll have to arrive in Arizona rested and in top form. Wouldn't you agree?"

"Custis, you should have been a snake oil peddler."

Longarm let out a laugh. "Boss, I like bein' a federal marshal. So how about some travel and ticket money? First class and round trip. Oh, and I'll need to buy a horse when I get off the train. I doubt that there will be much in the way of stagecoaches on the Navajo Reservation."

"Probably won't be," Billy had to agree. He scowled. "All right, Custis. Dammit, I'll ask someone else to do your paperwork. But you'd better keep me posted every step of the way after you reach the Navajo Reservation."

"Sure," Longarm said. "I'll just send a telegram from the reservation every evenin'. "I'm sure that's not goin' to be a problem in Monument Valley, given that it's so crowded with white folks and there are tradin' posts every mile or two."

"Don't be a smartass, Custis. Nobody likes a smart-ass."

Longarm popped out of his desk chair. "Boss, I'd really like to carry on this conversation, but I'm a bit short on time. So I'll swing by here in about an hour for the travel money, and I might as well take that letter you have from Miss Veronica right now."

"I'd rather you didn't."

"Why?" Longarm asked, genuinely puzzled.

"If someone on the Navajo Reservation happened to find it on you, it would almost certainly spell your doom. I see no point in you taking that risk. You can read it in full when you come back in an hour, and I'm sure you'll remember all the pertinent information."

"I'm sure," Longarm said, bounding off with a backward wave of his hand. "And don't tell Marshal Joe Timmons that you changed your mind about givin' me this Navajo assignment instead of him."

"Believe me, I won't."

Longarm was smiling from ear to ear as he went out the door. Action! That was what he craved, and there was nothing more that he enjoyed than the prospect of saving a beautiful former governor's daughter in distress.

Chapter 2

Longarm fairly danced out of the Federal Building on his way to his apartment. He wasn't blind to the dangers of going onto the huge Navajo Reservation, and he knew that his presence would be met with hostility and suspicion. Even so, Longarm had been on the reservation a time or two, and the prospect of visiting stunning Monument Valley, with all its red buttes and towers, was appealing. Also, he recalled how beautiful Miss Veronica was, and there was always the possibility that he would be able to render her a great service. In such cases, it was not entirely implausible that she would be grateful for his assistance and reward him in a manner that would be more valuable and bring far more pleasure than money.

"Excuse me?" a trembling voice said as a hand tugged at his coat sleeve. "Aren't you Marshal Custis Long?"

He turned to see a small, badly dressed woman in her early thirties holding the side of her swollen face with one hand while trying to fight back tears. Her lips were bleeding and it was clear she was going to have a black eye.

"I'm Marshal Long," he said with concern. "What happened to your poor face?"

"My husband, Horace, is drunk again, and when he gets drunk he gets mean and takes it out on me. He's in that saloon over there and he'll be spending all our rent money."

The woman started to cry, and when she wrapped her arms around Longarm's waist, he hugged and comforted her. "Now, now. Everything is going to be all right."

"But it won't all right a'tall if he spends our rent on drink! Why, last month after Horace went drinkin', we had to scrape by for weeks with almost nothing to eat."

"You are too thin," Longarm said, anger building way down in his gut. "Dear woman, what is your name?"

"Mildred. Mildred Gall. And my husband's name is. . . ."

"Horace Gall."

"And he's in the Red Jug Saloon?"

"Aye! And he'll stay there until every dime we have is gone."

"All right," Longarm said, glancing at his pocket watch and deciding that he would have to make quick work of this messy affair. "What does your husband look like?"

"Oh, he's real big and has a black beard. Horace wears a bowler and suspenders, and he likes to fight when he's drunk." Mildred lifted her chin with a little bit of pride. "Horace brags that he's never been whipped."

"Maybe that's because he picks on women like you."

"He fights men, too."

"Why does your husband fight?"

"Oh, he was once a bare-knuckles contender. Fought in England and Ireland, he did. and he was quite the figure in his prime."

Longarm scowled. If Horace was a former bare-knuckles fighter, that meant he wouldn't go down easy. And the last thing that Longarm wanted or needed was to have half of his face torn off in a bad fight with a tough opponent. In a stand-up, toe-to-toe slugfest, Horace might prove to be more than a match for Longarm.

"Miss Gall, does your husband carry a gun or a knife?"

"No gun."

"But he does carry a knife?"

"Aye. In his boot top. Right one. It's a big knife, too."

"All right," Longarm said, eyeing the saloon across the street. "I'll go in and have a word with the man."

"You need to be real careful. Horace has a quick and terrible temper."

Longarm took the little woman's arm and guided her across the street, then stopped on the boardwalk in front of the saloon. He removed his nice coat and hat, then rolled up his sleeves. "Miss Gall, I want you to stand right here until I come out with your husband in tow."

"Maybe . . . maybe I shouldn't have troubled you, Marshal Long." Mildred looked scared and she tried to hand back the coat and hat to Longarm. "Why don't you just go on about your business and I'll . . ."

"You'll what?" Longarm asked, trying to hide his impatience. "Go into that saloon and try to drag your big, bullying husband out before he spends all your rent money?"

"Well, I . . ." She scrubbed away tears. "I don't know. But I'll likely think of something."

"I'll bring him out," Longarm said, reaching across his waist to check the pistol he carried on the left side, butt forward.

"You aren't going to *shoot* my Horace, are you?"

"No."

"Promise?"

"I promise." Longarm took a deep breath. "Big man with a black beard and a knife in his right boot top. Anything else you want to tell me before I go in there after him?"

"He's bald," she said, "but he's vain about it, and that's why he always wears that bowler cocked a little over his right eye. And Horace is wearin' a black bandana tied around his neck."

"I'll bring him right out," Longarm said with more confidence than he actually felt. "And I'll see that Horace understands that a real man doesn't beat up on his wife and drink his family into ruin."

"If you could do that, I'd be forever in your debt." Mildred made the mistake of trying to smile, but winced at the pain. "Marshal, I clean and cook for those that either can't or don't have the time for it. I'd clean your place for free if you could just talk to my Horace and make him stop hitting me and drinkin' away all our money."

"We might make some arrangements on that," Longarm said while rolling up his sleeves.

She laid a hand on his arm and squeezed it. "Now, Marshal Long, you mustn't try and fight with Horace. You're a big man all right, but not nearly as big as my husband."

"Okay," Longarm said. "I'll just talk to the man and make him come out and apologize to you for the beating he gave, and then promise never to do it again or to get drunk and squander all your money."

"If you could do all that. . . ." Mildred took a deep, ragged breath. "If you could do all that, then I'd be willin' to repay you with *anything* I have that you might like."

She looked straight into Longarm's eyes and her meaning was crystal clear. "Thanks, but I'd just be doin' my job. This shouldn't take long."

"Oh," she said, "it won't take long a'tall. In ten seconds . . . maybe less . . . one of you will be stretched out on the floor, out cold."

Longarm took a deep breath and headed through the bat-wing doors of the notorious Red Jug Saloon. The minute he filled the doorway, conversation fell silent. There were about twenty men in the saloon, most of them leaning on a long, badly scarred bar. Cigar smoke was so thick it could have been cut and served on a plate. Longarm knew that this saloon was one of the worst in downtown Denver and was famous for its brawls that ended in death.

"Hello," Longarm said, standing just inside the saloon. "Can a man get a cold beer in this place?"

"Do bears shit in the forest?" the bartender called back. "Of course, you can! Step up to the bar and show me your money, Marshal Long."

"So you recognize me," Longarm said, dropping coins on the bar top.

"Oh, I recognize you, all right," the bartender, a short, heavyset man with muttonchop whiskers said with no friendliness. "You're the law, even though I don't see a badge pinned on your chest."

"I come here as an ordinary citizen," Longarm replied. "I'm not here to arrest anyone, so everyone can rest easy."

That settled, the conversation resumed and Longarm got his tall schooner of beer. He took a swallow, then watched and listened as his eyes adjusted to the dim and smoky saloon. He had learned long ago that a man didn't just walk out of broad daylight and into semidarkness and expect to be able to see a punch, a knife's blade or a bullet coming his way. No, it was always better to give one's eyes a few minutes' time to adjust and then make a move.

And as the minutes passed, his vision grew better and he saw the man that had to be Horace Gall. How could you miss such an ugly mountain of humanity? Horace was at least six-foot-six and as broad across the shoulders as an ordinary doorway. He was loud, too. When Gall laughed, his voice drowned out everything. And right now he was telling some ribald story to several men crowded around him.

With Monument Valley, Arizona, on his mind, Longarm knew that he had very little time to waste on this mission of mercy. He took another swig of beer and then carried his heavy mug over to where Gall was holding court.

"Horace?"

Gall was right at the point of delivering his punch line, and when Longarm interrupted him, he was not pleased. For a moment he tried to ignore Longarm, and then Longarm pushed one of the men in his audience aside and said, "You're Horace Gall and you're a gaw-damn wife beater and degenerate drunkard."

"What did you say!"

"You heard me, you overgrown piece of dog shit."

The room felt so silent that you could have heard a mouse let loose with a soft fart. Horace Gall was not a man accustomed to being challenged or insulted, and so he blinked several times while his brain slowly proc-essed what he'd just heard.

Suddenly, it was as if a bell had gone off deep inside his thick Neanderthal-like skull, and he bellowed, "Why, you . . ."

Longarm hurled the contents of his mug, half filled with beer, straight into Gall's ugly face. At the same time his left hand drove a thundering uppercut to the giant's body.

Gall's cheeks puffed outward and his breath exploded from his mouth. Longarm, with the empty beer glass still in his hand, slashed it down hard against the giant's temple. Gall dropped to both knees and Longarm stepped back and kicked him in the head just under his heavy jaw.

"Get up, Wife Beater," Longarm ordered. "And let's see how you fight men instead of women."

Amazingly, Gall wobbled to his feet, face bloody and eyes glazed. "What the hell are you doin' this for!"

"For your wife, Mildred!" Longarm threw another punch at the man's jaw, but Gall's huge arm was sud-denly in the way, blocking his punch, and then a fist from nowhere hit Longarm in the chest so hard that he spilled over a table and hit the floor.

"Now *you* get up!" Gall roared, wiping blood and beer

from his face. "Get up on your feet so I can kill you without even botherin' to bend over."

Longarm's chest felt as if it had been kicked by a big Missouri mule, and he wondered if Horace Gall had actually broken his sternum or knocked his ribs loose from their connections. Gawd! Longarm had never been hit so hard in his life.

Longarm came to his feet and knew in his gut that Mildred had been right to warn him not to try to stand toe-to-toe with this monstrous freak of nature. All right then, the man might be an animal on two legs, but his skull was only made of bone, and it would crack under the barrel of a heavy pistol.

Gall rushed Longarm and, if he hadn't tripped over a chair's leg, the giant might have reached his target. But when Horace Gall tripped, Longarm whipped out his gun and brought it crashing down on the man's forehead with far more force than he would ordinarily have used to pistol-whip a man.

"Ahhh!" Gall cried, hitting the floor and then trying to climb back to his feet. His bowler had fallen off his head, which was shiny with sweat.

Longarm let the man get halfway up and then he struck him again with the heavy barrel of his Colt. Gall collapsed to the sawdust, and while any ordinary man would have been out cold, this one reached down into his boot, drew out a knife and actually hurled it at Longarm. It seemed impossible that anyone could hurl a knife with any force or accuracy while on the floor, but Gall did it, and the move was so unexpected and amazing that the knife stuck Longarm in the side just over his belt. The blade was long and sharp, and the pain was excruciating. Longarm staggered backward, tearing the knife from his side just as someone from the crowd tossed Gall a pistol.

"Don't!" Longarm shouted in warning.

But Horace Gall wasn't going to listen to reason. He snatched the gun from the sawdust floor and took aim an instant before Longarm's own pistol was belching smoke and fire.

Two bullets on a downward trajectory punctured the shiny bald dome and exited out the back of the giant's massive skull. Gall dropped facedown in the sawdust, his body twitching all the way down to his boots.

"You killed him!" a man shouted. "You killed Horace Gall!"

Longarm clamped his left hand over the knife wound. He knew that it wasn't fatal, but he was losing blood, and the pain in his side coupled with the pain in the center of his chest where Gall had nearly torn apart his rib cage was so intense that he felt woozy.

"Which one of you sonsabitches threw him that pistol?" Longarm demanded, eyes searing the crowd of rough-and-ready drinkers. "Who did it!"

No one offered a word, and Longarm knew that whoever had tossed Gall the pistol would never come forth and face certain arrest and jail time.

Longarm took a deep, steadying breath, then staggered over to the dead giant and used the toe of his boot to turn the body onto its back. He rifled through Gall's pockets, pulling out maybe a month's worth of rent in cash. Then he took the pistol that was clenched in the dead man's hand and stuck it behind his gun belt.

"Gall's widow is outside waiting for me with a face

that is black and blue from this bastard's fists," he said to
no one in particular. "Gall was a wife beater and when
he got me with a knife he was facing prison . . . or worse.
If I knew who it was that tossed this gun to him . . . I'd
see that man sent to prison for a long, long time. But
now the wife gets the gun to sell for food money and
this cash I took will go for her rent money. Anyone have
any objections to that?"

No one said a word.

"Good!" Longarm hissed. "I have no gawdamn use
for a man who mistreats women, children, dogs or horses.
No use at all!"

"Who's going to pay for Horace Gall's burial?" the
bartender shouted across the hushed room.

"I guess you sonsabitches had better pay the bill,"
Longarm said. "Either that, or toss him in the back alley
and let the mongrel dogs eat his stinking carcass."

Longarm turned for the door and tried to walk up-
right, but he was hurting so much that he didn't do a
very good job of it.

"Marshal Long, you're a hard man!" someone from
the crowd behind him got up enough courage to yell.
"And lawmen aren't welcome in this saloon!"

Longarm wheeled around at the doorway. "Whoever
said that needs to be man enough to step apart from the
others and come forward right now."

No one moved or spoke a word. But Longarm knew
that one of them was feeling like a coward, and that
pleased him mightily.

"Horace Gall deserved to die. And if you don't believe it, then come outside and take a look at his wife's
battered face."

Longarm waited a moment and then he turned his back on the crowd and limped outside into the clean air to stand on the boardwalk.

"My gawd!" Mildred Gall cried, when she saw the blood on his shirt. "What happened!"

"Your husband could hit harder than any man I ever met," Longarm told her. "But he won't ever do it again."

Mildred's hand flew to her mouth and her eyes grew round and big. Longarm reached into his pocket and dragged out all the cash that he'd taken from her husband's body, then he took some out of his wallet to add to the pot. "Here. This ought to get you by for awhile. "

She took the money.

"And take this gun, too," Longarm said.

But Mildred backed away, her face grim and bloodless. "Is that the gun that you used to kill my husband!"

"No, it's the one that someone tossed to him so he could kill me."

"I don't want it."

"Take it anyway," Longarm said roughly. "Go to the gun shop and sell it for cash. Between what it will bring and the cash you have now, you should be all right for a couple of months at least."

"And then what will I do with Horace gone?" she demanded.

"Buy a couple of nice dresses. Let your face heal and make yourself pretty again. Then find a *good* husband."

"It won't be that easy, Marshal!" she said, her voice filled with anger and no small measure of despair.

"Nothin' in life is easy," Longarm told Mildred Gall. "But you're fortunate in that decent women are in the minority out in the West. Don't you go drinkin' or whorin', and you'll soon find a good man. Given what you had, almost any man will be an improvement."

"When he was sober, Horace *was* a good man."

"Well," Longarm said, his hand clamping tight on his knife wound, "I find that hard to believe. But you do as you please with the new lease on life I've just given you."

"You promised me that you wouldn't kill my husband, Marshal Long!"

"And I wouldn't have if your husband hadn't knifed and then tried to put a bullet into me. He was the hardest fighter I've ever been up against, but he made a fatal mistake when he went from fists to guns."

Longarm headed up the street, unaware that the drinkers had emptied the Red Jug Saloon and had heard his words and were watching him. He didn't hear the bartender say after looking at the poor, beaten little woman, "The marshal was right. Gall deserved what he got! Now how about we take up a collection for the little widow and then drag that bastard's big carcass out into the back alley for the dogs?"

There was a murmur of agreement as the men of the Red Jug Saloon dug into their pockets and a hat was passed all around.

Chapter 3

Custis was bent over sideways and in considerable pain using his key to unlock his apartment door. The good news was that his wound had stopped bleeding and he knew from experience it would scab over and heal, given a little time and medical attention. The bad news was that he'd ruined his shirt, vest and suit coat with his blood.

"Custis! What on earth happened to you!"

He turned to see his friend and lover, Molly Malloy, poking her head out of her adjacent hallway door. Molly was always watching out for him, and she cooked a lot of his meals. In turn, he bought her flowers and perfume and took her out to dinner on the town at least once a week. Molly made no bones about the fact that it was her sworn intention to get Longarm to marry her someday, but he had always told her that he was not the marrying kind. Trouble was, Molly didn't take him serious enough on that particular point.

"Custis, you're bleeding!"

"It's stopped, I think."

"What on earth happened to you?"

"I got in a real bad fight over at the Red Jug Saloon," he explained. "The man got me with a knife and I finally had no choice but to shoot him in the head."

"Let me help you get that blood-soaked shirt, vest and coat off. I should send someone for a doctor."

"I don't have time for a doctor. This is just a flesh wound that will soon heal."

Molly Malloy began to help Longarm out of his clothes. "These are completely ruined," she said, undressing him and then finding a washcloth to gently wipe the dried blood away. "You need this to be stitched up properly by a doctor."

"I've got to catch a train out of Denver this afternoon without fail."

"Not today you're not," she told him. "Maybe tomorrow if you. . . ."

Longarm put his hands on the pretty woman's shoulders. "Molly, I *have* to get out to the Arizona Territory, and I need to start traveling today. Now please pour me a glass of whiskey and help me get cleaned up and dressed for the train."

She looked into his eyes and saw that he was not going to change his mind. "All right, you big stubborn bastard. But at least you can tell me what happened and why you are in such a hot hurry to leave town."

"Pour us whiskey," he said, "and I'll give you the short version of a very long and mysterious story."

"Fair enough," she said. "Now lie down and rest while I get the whiskey poured."

Longarm slumped onto his bed without a stitch of

clothing. He closed his eyes and listened to Molly rushing around in his tiny kitchen and heard the clink of glass on glass as she poured him a stout drink and no doubt a second one for herself. Molly, he thought, was a fine, pretty and competent woman. A man could do a whole lot worse than marrying someone exactly like her.

"Here," she said, pushing a pillow under his head and then handing him a glass. "Drink it all down, because that wound has to be stitched. I'm going to my apartment for a thread and needle."

"Do you really think it won't heal by itself with just some bandaging?" he asked, gulping whiskey and feeling the heat of it all the way down into the pit of his belly.

"Custis, I know this is not what you want to hear, but that knife wound needs to be stitched or the scab might very well break loose on the train and then you'd have one hell of a mess. I've done it before and I'm good at it. It will hurt like hell but it won't take long."

"All right," he conceded. "But I really don't have a whole lot of time."

"I'll call you a horse and buggy and you'll be at the train station in plenty of time. Besides, you know the damned Denver and Rio Grande never leaves on time. It's usually at least an hour late."

"Be my bad luck for it to leave Denver right on schedule today."

Molly just scowled and said, "Drink that whiskey and pour yourself another glass. I'll be back in two minutes!"

Longarm heard his door slam shut and he figured if Molly really was going to stitch up that knife wound, he'd better have a strong belt of whiskey working in his veins in order to mute the pain.

Molly was back before he could pour a second glass. She poured it for him and then said, "Lay your head back on the pillow and close your eyes. Try to think of something pleasant and I'll have this wound stitched up tight in no time at all."

"I'll think about making love to you," he said with a wink and a brave smile.

"You do that, Big Boy."

"Ouch!" he said, tossing another gulp of whiskey down, swallowing it and then grinding his teeth. "What are you using on me? A darning needle?"

"Just a sharp little needle is all," she answered. "This wound is going to take at least six stitches. If that knife had hit you about two inches further inward, you'd be a goner."

"I know. The guy I fought was named Horace Gall and he was a big, vicious bastard. I had him down and out on his back, and I'll never know how he threw a knife so straight and hard from the floor, but he did. Then he tried to shoot me with a gun that some fool in the crowd tossed him, but I shot him first."

Molly sighed. "One of these days you won't come out of a fight alive. Why don't you find another line of work and marry me, Custis? I'd make you a good wife. I like making love and you know I'm a pretty good cook."

"I know you would make any man a fine wife, but I'm just not ready to settle down."

"Will you ever be?"

"Most likely not," he confessed. "You need to find another man."

She jabbed the needle angrily into his flesh and finished her stitching. Then she surprised him by grabbing his flaccid manhood. "I get exasperated by your independence, Custis, but I know that I'll never find another man with a donger this size."

"Oh, I dunno," he said, smiling and taking a gulp of whiskey. "You just might."

"Nope. I've had my share of men, but you're the best lover I ever had. So how about a little ride for Molly before you head off on that train?"

Longarm couldn't believe he'd heard her correctly. "Are you serious! I'm lying here in pain and you're asking me to give you a poke?"

"Yeah. That's what I'm asking in return for the stitches and for being so loyal and thinking you might change your mind about marrying me someday."

"Jeez, Molly. I couldn't . . ."

"This won't take long," she promised, taking his manhood in her mouth and then beginning to work his big rod up and down with her lips and her tongue.

"Molly," he said, draining his whiskey and suddenly feeling a whole lot better than he had when he'd staggered into his apartment. "I can't believe you'd want to do this, given the circumstances."

She tongued the head of his stiff cock. "How long will you be gone from me and Denver this time?"

"I have no idea."

"Well then, I want you to remember me when you're off someplace risking your scarred-up hide. I want you to remember how Molly did you right just before she dressed and sent you off to the train station."

Longarm was standing tall and wet. "I'll remember.

Nobody ever did it to me any better than you, Molly. I really mean that."

"Of course you do," she said, enthusiastically working on his tool and then standing up to pull off her dress. "Now you're going to give little Molly a good ride."

"Be careful of those new stitches."

"Oh, I will. Believe me, I will!"

Molly was slender and athletic enough to lower herself down on Longarm's rod and then gently but firmly begin to satisfy her own considerable lust. In a few minutes, she was furiously working her muscular little bottom up and down and Longarm was feeling no pain whatsoever. When he erupted like a little volcano, Molly was right there with him, hollering and hooting with pleasure.

Spent of her passion, she sagged forward, kissed his bruised face and said, "Be careful, my sweet man. And come back to me whole, horny and handsome."

"I'll do my best," he said, grinning foolishly. "Now you'd better get off and help me get dressed and packed for the trip."

"Sure," she said, gently extracting herself with a big smile on her wet lips.

With Molly's help, Longarm was bandaged, scrubbed down with a warm, damp washrag, then dressed in clean clothes and ready to leave in a half hour. "How do I look?" he asked her at the door as he picked up his traveling bag.

"You look like a well-satisfied man," Molly told him. "But I sure wish you didn't have to leave today. You're handsome as ever, but the lines in your face tell me that you're still in some pain and that you're exhausted."

"It was a hard fight that I was in today, but great love-making. Both take something out of a man."

"I'm sure that they do," she said, coming over to wrap her arms around his neck. "What would you do if I told you that you made me pregnant today?"

Longarm dropped his bag, shivered and gulped. "What in tarnation caused you to say a thing like that?"

"Oh, I don't know," she replied. "But women do get pregnant, and I'm not making love to any other men."

"Molly, I . . ."

She pressed a forefinger over his lips. "Don't you worry about it, Custis. I was just asking out of curiosity, that's all."

He sighed. "Okay, but you really had me going for a moment there."

"You'll recover. Try to get some sleep on the train trip west to Arizona."

"My boss has promised me a first-class ticket."

"Then this must be a very important assignment."

"It is," he said, not willing to take the time to fully explain. "If I get a chance, I'll send you a letter or two."

"No, you won't," Molly told him, "but that's all right. I'll be here when you return."

Longarm picked up his bag, kissed Molly and headed out of his door. "You take care of yourself as well," he said over his shoulder as he lurched down the hallway.

"Oh, Custis, I forgot to summon a horse and buggy."

"I'll catch one out on the street. After making love to you, my legs feel a little weak."

"So do mine!"

She blew him a kiss and went back into his apartment. Longarm knew that she would sleep many nights in his bed rather than in her own right next door. Molly Malloy just liked to do that for some odd, feminine reason that he knew that he'd never understand.

Chapter 4

Riding first class on the railroad was a rare treat for Longarm. Along with a much-appreciated bed to lie on, he
enjoyed the fine meals and good wine offered in the
railroad's dining car. So after several days of resting and
feasting, Longarm was almost disappointed to hear the
porter shout, "Next stop is Holbrook, Arizona Territory.
All passengers for Holbrook, prepare to disembark!"

Longarm stretched, yawned and gathered his few belongings, packing them neatly in a heavy canvas bag with
leather straps that had served him well over the years.

"Why are you getting off here, Marshal?" the porter
asked when Longarm emerged from his sleeping car.
"Flagstaff would be a whole lot cooler and greener."

"Bert, you know by now that I go where I'm sent,"
Longarm told the porter, tipping him five dollars for the
many services he'd provided on this journey westward.
"But being as how this is summer and it's hot, you're

right about the fact that I'd have preferred to be sent somewhere cooler."

As the train slowed, Longarm stuck his head out and gazed at the little railroad town just up ahead. Holbrook wasn't much to look at, but the surrounding country was starkly beautiful with its red buttes and broken cliffs dotted with the short, blue gray pinion pine and juniper trees. Some people called this the Land of the Painted Desert, and Longarm could see why: the crumbling rocks and dirt were as colorful as anything to be found in the West. What was also quite interesting were the petrified logs that they'd passed only a few miles back. Longarm had told Molly Malloy that out in eastern Arizona there was an entire forest of ancient trees that had somehow turned to stone, but she hadn't believed him. Yet these trees were everywhere, some giant in size, made all the more impressive because you could clearly see their hard and red mineralized bark.

Many of the locals broke off and collected pieces of this amazing rock, and some even polished them so that you could actually see the tree rings. Even now, as Longarm prepared to get off the train, he could see people hawking specimens of the petrified rock to the passengers who were going to stretch their legs while the train took on more coal and water.

"Maybe I'll be seeing you on the trip back," Bert said, patting Longarm on the shoulder as he stepped down on the train station's platform. "You be careful around this part of Arizona. I hear that there is a lot of trouble between the Navajo and the federal government brewin' up on the reservation."

"Maybe I can do something about that," Longarm said.

"And maybe you'll get your scalp lifted," Bert called. "Be careful on that Navajo Reservation, Marshal Long. I want to enjoy your generous tips on the train back to Denver."

Longarm waved back over his shoulder and walked into a town whose population was about half white and half Indian. Holbrook was a prosperous looking railroad town, and there was a line of tall cottonwoods still standing along a dry wash that ran full in the springtime. Half a dozen businesses lined both sides of the street, and two of them were hotels. Longarm chose the Hancock Hotel because its exterior had a fresh coat of white paint and the establishment looked more respectable and clean. The hotel had a nice covered front porch where several men were smoking and sipping whiskey.

"Afternoon, gents!" Longarm called as he approached the hotel. "How are things going today?"

"Could be better . . . but they could be a helluva lot worse. Things will probably get worse before they get better," a dapper man who was probably a traveling salesman or gambler answered with a wink and a smile.

The three other men that were sitting with him laughed and Longarm dropped his bag on the boardwalk. "Is this hotel clean and the beds free of mites and fleas?"

"No," another man said, "but at least the mites and fleas in their beds ain't as hungry as they are in the Castor Hotel across the street. And Miss Allie sets a fine table for just a dollar a day on top of the room cost. Mister, you won't do any better in Holbrook."

"Thanks for the recommendation," Longarm said, tipping his hat. "I'll go inside and get a room."

"After you get settled, come on out and we'll find

you a chair and a glass. Maybe you'd enjoy our company and we can lie about as well as anyone you could possibly hope to find in this town."

"I'll do that."

"And," the dapper man said, winking, "if you're in a hurry for a little lady to ease your joints, all you have to do is ask Miss Allie. She's the owner of this hotel and she means to make her boarders happy."

"I'll keep that in mind," Longarm told them as he went inside.

There was a buxom blonde, wearing a lot of turquoise and silver jewelry, smoking a thin cigar behind the registration desk. She was intently reading a newspaper and sipping a steaming cup of coffee. Longarm judged her to be about forty and still good looking, although she was starting to show a little age and wear like everyone else.

"Are you Miss Allie, the owner of this hotel?" Longarm asked, looking around at the well-appointed lobby and an open doorway with a sign that read: GOOD FOOD AND DRINK FOR HOTEL GUESTS ONLY.

She glanced up from her newspaper and eyed Longarm for a moment before she smiled. "Say, handsome, you looking for a room and a bed with or without a frisky woman?"

"A bed *without* a woman will be fine for tonight."

"How disappointing," she said, laying down her paper and blowing a lazy smoke ring in his direction. "Why, as big and handsome as you are, I might have been interested in doin' a little bed-bouncin' myself."

Allie chortled and Longarm blushed a little bit. "How much for a room?"

"One dollar for the room and another for the best supper you'll find in this poor old railroad town."

"That's kinda steep, isn't it?"

"I serve the best steaks in Arizona and good red wine with your evening meal. I don't provide a midday meal, but after you finish the huge breakfast I serve, you won't be hungry all day. And my rooms are clean and the beds won't give you bug bites or the scabies."

Longarm nodded, beginning to think that maybe it would be worth two dollars.

"However, if you're short on funds and want to save a dollar a day, just go on over to the Castor Hotel across the street and see what you get for your money. No meals. No wine. An ugly, diseased whore and bedbug bites so bad you'll think you slept on an ant hill all night."

"I'm sold," Longarm said. "But I have no idea if I'll be spending more than just this one night."

"Then pay me the two dollars and I'll give you a key to room eight, which is the first door upstairs on the right. It overlooks the street out in front and you'll enjoy a nice evening breeze if you leave your door open until you retire for the night. Fifty cents more gets you a hot bath."

"Sounds good, and I'll take the bath." Longarm laid two and a half dollars down on the desk.

"Supper is at six and I like my guests all to be sitting at the table at the same time. Makes it one hell of a lot easier on the kitchen help and the cook."

"Do you join us at the table?"

"I do, and I'll tolerate no tobacco spitting, farting, cussing or complaining. I like a good conversation and

I'll tell you right away that I can't abide whiners or drunks . . . but you don't look like either."

"I'm not."

"Sign my registration book and I'll give you your room key."

Longarm signed his name and place of residence as Denver. He left the space asking for occupation blank.

"What do you do for a living?" Allie asked.

"I work for the federal government."

"Oh, shit!" Allie made a face. "Mister, are you another Indian agent come to town to fix the problems we have and will always have up on the Navajo Reservation?"

"Nope."

Longarm took his key before the woman could ask any more questions and headed up the stairs. It wasn't that he tried to hide his lawman profession, it was just that he had learned from hard experience that it was better if he kept his business his own business.

Room eight was even nicer than expected. There were lace curtains, original oil paintings of the Painted Desert on the walls and a big Navajo blanket that served as a rug on a clean and dust-free wooden floor. Longarm pitched his bag in the corner and stretched out on the bed to take its measure. Before he knew it, he was dozing.

"Hey in there!" came Allie's voice. "It's almost six o'clock and I haven't seen or heard a word from you since you came up here. You asleep?"

Longarm sat up and yawned. "Not anymore."

"Get dressed if you're naked and come on down to

join us all at my table. I told you I expected all my guests to eat at the same time."

"I'll be right down, Miss Allie."

"You didn't even take a bath yet."

"I'll do it in the morning, if that is all right."

"Sure. But I like my guests to be clean when they turn in for the night."

"Then I'll take my bath right after supper."

"That's a good idea," Allie said. "How do you like your steak cooked?"

"Pretty rare."

"Good man. I like pink meat! Is your meat pink?"

Allie giggled and was gone before Longarm could even begin to come up with a reply.

There were five men waiting at the table, with Miss Allie seated at the head nearest to the kitchen. When Longarm sat down, everyone bowed their head and Miss Allie offered a quick prayer. "Bless this food and those that eat it and those that cooked it. And bless those that haven't enough money to stay at my hotel and have to sleep across the street in that flea-infested dump the Castor Hotel. And bless the beasts who gave up their bodies so that we could eat their meat! Amen."

As soon as the prayer was over, everyone dug into the serving bowls of food, forking huge, juicy steaks onto their plates along with mashed potatoes, gravy, peas and corn and plenty of freshly baked sourdough bread. There were six bottles of red wine on the table, and those were quickly grabbed as the guests raised their glasses in a toast, shouting, "To Miss Allie!"

Miss Allie was dressed up for her dinner guests. She wore a lacy collar and a string of pearls around her neck that would have been the envy of a rich Denver woman. Her blonde hair was fixed in a swirl, and she had applied makeup and lipstick. She looked every inch a lady of means, and after the toast, the table's conversation was lively and stimulating.

"What the Navajo ought to do is just settle down and quit trying to stir up trouble," one of the diners said. "It doesn't look like they've learned a thing at all, given the defeats they and the other Indians have suffered. Good heavens, they're being fed, clothed and educated, and all their medical needs are being met by the government. And we all know that means that we the taxpayers are footing the bill."

"Ah, yes," another man added, "but they were far better off before we white folks arrived and displaced them and killed off their buffalo."

"I disagree. How in the hell do you know they were better off if we weren't here yet to see that they were better off?"

"No cussing," Miss Allie warned, giving the man a disapproving frown. "You know the rules, Mr. Benjamin."

"Sorry, Miss Allie. I guess I got carried away for a minute."

The lively dinner conversation moved back and forth between the "Navajo problem," as they were all calling it, and the rumor that a big gold strike had been found on the reservation by a man named Fergus Horn.

"I hear that Mr. Horn was married to the daughter of the governor of Colorado," a fellow named Albert commented. "Can you imagine that?"

"Fergus Horn is a very handsome man," Allie said, looking around the table. "He's stayed here at my hotel many times, and he's always been a gentleman. He's a real charmer. Very intelligent and quite a dashing fellow. He looks like and reminds me of our newest guest, Mr. Custis Long."

"I hear that Mr. Horn was a United States Marshal before he came to this territory and started stirring up the Navajo."

"That's what I heard as well," another man said around a mouth stuffed with steak. "And from what I hear, this Fergus Horn has shot three men up near Monument Valley for no other reason than that he likes to see men die!"

Mr. Benjamin said, "I think Fergus Horn ought to be shot himself before he gets the whole Navajo Nation stirred up and on the warpath. Why, there are enough Navajo to ride into Holbrook and wipe out this whole town!"

Allie caught Longarm's eye, and he could see that she was amused rather than upset by this heated debate. "Mr. Long," she said, looking at him with more than a casual interest, "I'd be very interested to know what *you* think about this trouble we're having up north around Monument Valley"

"I don't know much about it," Longarm said when all eyes turned to him. "But it sounds quite serious."

"Oh," Albert said, shaking his fork at Longarm, "it's far more than just serious. I sadly predict that we're going to have a lot of blood spilled on both sides before the dust over Monument Valley settles. And who is to say that the fighting and killing won't spread all the way down here to Holbrook and south through the Mormon settlements?"

"That's right!" another man cried. "This trouble and this cancer named Fergus Horn has to be nipped in the bud before it gets completely out of hand and innocent people both red and white are killed."

"Mr. Long," Miss Allie said, raising her hand for silence, "is from Denver, Colorado, and he works for the federal government. Isn't that right?"

"It is," Longarm said, not wanting the conversation to center on himself. "But—"

"And so," Miss Allie gently interrupted, "I have to assume that you know about Fergus Horn and the governor's daughter that he married and brought out here to the Arizona Territory."

"I probably don't know any more about Mr. Horn and his wife than the rest of you," Longarm said, concentrating on his plate.

"Maybe you're just being modest," Miss Allie suggested. "What *exactly* do you do for the federal government?"

Longarm always avoided that question but when he was cornered he refused to lie. "I'm a United States Marshal."

"Well, I'll be gawdamned!" a short, fat man named Arthur exclaimed. "You're a federal marshal and you've just arrived in Holbrook? Then surely you've come to help settle this trouble!"

Longarm finished swallowing a bite of steak and said, "I was sent to investigate the problem and try to find a peaceful solution."

"Were you well acquainted with Marshal Fergus Horn?"

"I knew the man."

"Do you know his wife?" Miss Allie pressed. "Her name is Veronica and she is quite beautiful."

"I've met her a few times in Denver," Longarm admitted. "By the way, this steak is excellent and the wine is superb. Would someone pass down that bottle of cabernet?"

The bottle was passed to Longarm, who studiously refilled his glass, knowing that they were all staring at him.

"So what do you intend to do about this former associate of yours named Fergus Horn?" the dapper man that Longarm was now sure was a gambler asked, leaning back in his chair.

"I don't know yet. I was sent here to investigate, and that's what I mean to do, starting tomorrow."

"Will you be going right up to the northern part of the reservation?" Miss Allie asked.

"I will," Longarm replied. "But first I'll have to outfit myself. Rent a horse and buy supplies. Does anyone here have a recommendation for an honest horse trader?"

"I know one that I can well recommend," Allie said. "He's a half-breed named Ira, and he's honest. You're not only going to need a horse and supplies, you're going to need a competent guide. One that speaks fluent Navajo and really knows the country, the clans and all the families. If you don't have that person with you, Marshal, you aren't going to be of much use to anyone on the reservation."

"I'd like to speak to Ira first thing tomorrow morning," Longarm told his hostess. "I know that there is a good deal of unrest and trouble brewing on the reservation and there is not a day to be wasted."

"Ira has gone up to Sun Mountain on some spiritual matter," Allie said. "But he'll be back the day after tomorrow."

"I don't want to wait that long."

"You don't have any choice, Marshal Long. Ira is the only man who you'd be able to trust and who could keep you from getting ambushed out there in the big country to the north."

"But . . ."

"In the meantime," Allie said, "I'm sure that there are a few people right here in Holbrook you can discuss the problems we are facing with and who will offer you both help and excellent advice."

"I'll think about that and make the decision about Ira tomorrow morning," Longarm decided.

"One last question," Albert said. "Were you sent from Denver to arrest or to kill Fergus Horn?"

"I was not," Longarm said emphatically.

"Then were you sent to find Mrs. Veronica Horn, who has not been seen for months?"

"You said *one* question," Longarm told the man. "But you asked two questions and I'm going to decline to answer the second one. Now, because my official business is not something I can discuss, would everyone at this table please not ask me any more questions?"

"You heard the man," Miss Allie said to the others. "Mr. Long is my guest and I will not allow him to be badgered for information or questioned as if he were in court on a witness stand. So let's all just enjoy our meal and wine and have a nice time together."

"Thank you," Longarm said to the woman. "And I

sure am glad that I decided to stay and eat here at the Hancock Hotel instead of the one across the street."

"We are, too," Miss Allie said. "And I will send a rider out early tomorrow morning to find Ira and tell him he is needed back here as soon as he can possibly complete his ceremony."

"I know of a horse for sale right here in town," the gambler said. "He's a tall, good-looking sorrel horse that you might want to buy. He is being boarded at Polk's Stable, just up the street."

"I'd like to look at him," Longarm said. "Thanks for the tip."

"My pleasure. Mr. Polk just happens to owe me some money, and if you buy that horse then he can't say he's too broke to pay off the debt."

"I understand."

"Then you'll also understand why I'd like to join you when you go look at the sorrel."

"I'll be up early," Longarm told the man.

"I'll be ready to go when you are. My name is John Smith, and I'll meet you here at breakfast."

"Breakfast is at eight o'clock sharp," Miss Allie said to everyone.

"I won't be late again," Longarm told her.

"We'll see. We'll see," Miss Allie said with a crooked smile that told Longarm something private and possibly even seductive was very much on her mind.

Chapter 5

Longarm slept like a dead man that night, and when he awoke he shaved, took a bath and then quickly dressed and was just in time to sit down for breakfast at eight o'clock. The same five hotel guests and Miss Allie were sipping coffee and preparing to be served, but there was one other man in the room and he didn't look a bit happy.

"Marshal Long," Miss Allie said, coming to her feet and forcing a nervous smile. "It seems that after dinner last night one of our guests went saloon hopping and told everyone in town that you are in Holbrook on official business."

"Is that a fact?" Longarm drawled, giving each of the guests his steely eye.

"I'm afraid that it is," Miss Allie said, voice filled with disgust. "And that's why Marshal Brady Slocum is here this morning."

Longarm nodded and took the town marshal's measure. Brady Slocum was a large man, sloppy looking with a scraggly beard and deep-set, wary black eyes. He had a weak chin and jug ears, but there was something about his face that told Longarm the man was tough and calculating. Longarm had gone through this kind of situation many times before and he knew that Brady Slocum was suspicious and defensive about a federal lawman whose authority exceeded his own coming into Holbrook and making him look bad.

"Marshal Long," Slocum said, voice dripping with contempt, "when a federal marshal comes into my town, they ought to have the courtesy of coming directly to my office and introducing themselves to state their business ... if they really have any business."

It was clear that Brady Slocum wasn't going to be courteous or friendly, and he sure wasn't going to cooperate in a meaningful way so Longarm felt no obligation to apologize. "I was tired yesterday when I got off the train and I'm not required to visit you or anyone else on official federal business."

Slocum's face darkened. "Professional courtesy just doesn't seem to apply when it comes to you meddling feds."

"I think," Longarm said, his own anger starting to rise, "that we have nothing to talk about. So why don't you run along and swat some flies or scratch a stray dog while I enjoy my breakfast in peace."

"Gawdamn you!" Slocum exploded. "If you don't show me and my office a little respect, I'm going to feed you your breakfast, plate and all!"

Longarm had taken a chair, but now he came to his feet. "I'll be through eating in less than half an hour," he said. "And then I'm going to look at a horse to buy or rent at Polk's Stable. If you are looking for a fight, that's where you can find me. But if I were you, I'd think hard about that move."

"I don't need to think about it," Slocum said. "And I'll be at Polk's waiting for you. One half hour."

"It might be a little longer," Longarm said, taking pleasure in goading the man. "I might want to enjoy a second cup of coffee with the excellent company at this table."

Longarm sat back down, fixed his napkin in his shirt and said, "Would someone pass that plate of ham and eggs? It sure looks delicious."

Longarm wasn't paying any attention to the local marshal now, but he could feel hatred being sent in his direction.

"One half hour!" Brady Slocum hissed, stomping out of the room.

For a moment there was silence, and then Miss Allie said, "That man has been a thorn in my side since the day he took office four years ago. Brady Slocum is proud as a peacock, clever as a fox and mean as a diamondback rattlesnake. If you intend to go to the stable and meet him, you'd better be prepared for a hard, vicious fight."

"I already had one just before leaving Denver," Longarm said to no one in particular. "And I've got a stab wound in my side that is on the mend. The last thing I need is a fight."

"Then what are you going to do?" the gambler, John Smith, asked.

"I'll meet him at the stable and try to cool the man

down. If, however, Marshal Slocum insists on a fight, I'll make it my business to finish it quick."

The table guests exchanged skeptical glances and then silently began to eat. It was clear to Longarm that they thought he was making too light of this confrontation and that he might be in for a fearsome beating.

When breakfast was finished and Longarm had enjoyed his second cup of coffee, he checked the Colt strapped to his left side and stood up from the table. "Mr. Smith, let's go take a look at that sorrel gelding that you say would make me a good horse."

"Are you sure that's a good idea?"

"I thought you needed the sale money so you could have Mr. Polk pay you a debt."

"Well, I can always use extra money," the gambler said. "But last night lady luck favored me at cards and so this morning I'm feeling rather flush. That's the way it is with cards, you know. Today you're almost busted, to-morrow you're flying high. The point is, Marshal Long, that I don't have to have that money that you'd pay Mr. Polk right away and I'd prefer that you weren't hurt in a fight."

The explanation made Longarm feel good. "Mr. Smith, I sincerely appreciate your concern, but my job is to face up to trouble and handle it . . . however I can. Now, I didn't ask for a fight with your local marshal. He seems to have a bone in his craw and is forcing the is-sue. What kind of a federal officer of the law would I be if I dodged that kind of trouble?"

"I understand," Smith said, "but I have also seen

Marshal Slocum in a fight or two and he's always been unbeatable."

"No man is unbeatable," Longarm replied. "And besides that, he won't be losing face at the stable if he backs off."

"I think you're being overly optimistic on that point," the gambler said. "But you've been warned and I hope that this all works out fine."

"Marshal Slocum needs to be taken down a peg or two," Longarm said, loud enough for everyone at the table to hear. "He was right that I probably should have gone directly to his office from the train, but I didn't do that and he wouldn't let me apologize for that small mistake. Instead, Slocum came here angry and looking to insult me, or worse, and so our mistakes canceled each other out. Now it's time to see if the man is really mad enough to fight . . . or if he has cooled down and wants to be reasonable."

"I'd think perhaps I should come along," Miss Allie said.

"Not a chance," Longarm told her. "If anything, having a beautiful and prosperous woman at the stable would only ensure that the fool's pride would kick in and he'd insist on a fight."

"Be careful then," she warned. "Marshal Slocum carries a sock filled with buckshot and he uses it so that he doesn't injure his fists."

"He's right handed, isn't he?" Longarm asked.

"Yes, I believe that he is."

"Then I'll be ready for the sock, and I appreciate the warning." Longarm smiled at the hotel guests and tipped

his hat to Miss Allie. "Come along Mr. Smith, I'm eager
to take a look at that sorrel gelding."

The walk down to Polk's Stable was short and without
incident. When Longarm arrived at the stable, he saw a
bald and worried looking man standing in front of a big
barn, wringing the brim of his hat.

"That is Mr. Polk," Smith whispered. "How you doin'
today, John?"

"Not good. Not good at all," Polk replied. "Marshal
Brady Slocum is waiting inside the barn for your big
friend, and he's out for blood. I don't want any trouble
on my property. I think you should both go back to the
hotel until Marshal Slocum cools off a bit."

"Where is the sorrel horse that you have for sale?"
Longarm asked, ignoring the stable owner's advice.

"He's out back in a corral. Nicest horse I've had to
sell in quite some time."

"How old is he?"

"Oh," Polk said, "he's still pretty young. You can see
the cups in his teeth and so I'd judge him a four-year-
old . . . maybe five. And he's sound as a dollar and well
broke to ride."

"Have *you* ridden the animal?" Longarm asked, heading off around the barn to see the sorrel, with Smith and
Polk hurrying after him.

"No, I haven't," the stable owner admitted. "But I
have seen the horse ridden many times. He was owned
by a drunken Slash S cowboy who got shot down last
month right here in the street. Good cowboy and good
horse. Sure was a shame, but . . ."

"Who shot him?" Longarm asked.

"Marshal Slocum. The cowboy was blind drunk and firing his gun while racing that sorrel up and down the street. He was really raising hell, and when the marshal came out and told him to put away his gun and that he was under arrest, the cowboy got mad and spurred his horse right at Marshal Slocum. Would have run the marshal over except that Slocum drew his pistol, fired and shot the young cowboy straight through the heart."

"Marshal Slocum must be a pretty good man with his gun as well as his sap," Longarm said.

"Oh, you heard about that sock filled with buckshot that he carries, huh?" Polk said. "He's real good with that, too."

"Is that the horse you're offering for sale?" Longarm asked, rounding the barn and seeing two horses in a pole corral, one a fine sorrel and the other an ugly buckskin with saddle sores on its back.

"That's the one that the cowboy died on while racin' up and down the street. You can't fault the sorrel for what that poor foolish cowboy did to get himself ventilated."

"No," Longarm agreed, "you sure can't. Why don't you saddle and bridle the animal up and I'll take a ride to test him out?"

"You won't be able to ride after I'm finished beating the shit out of you," Marshal Brady Slocum said, emerging from inside the barn.

Longarm heaved a deep sigh. He had hoped that this man would just go away, but that now seemed not to be the case.

"You really don't want to fight with me," he said to the man as he approached.

"I disagree," Slocum said, knotting his big fists. "I never whipped a federal lawman before, and this is going to be a special treat."

"I don't think so," Longarm said, whipping out his Colt and pointing it at the town's lawman. "Hold up there and go on living . . . or keep coming and sign your own death warrant."

Marshal Slocum couldn't stop fast enough. "You'd shoot me down in cold blood?"

"I've got a bandage on my side from a knife wound," Longarm explained, gun held steady on the man. "So it would be dumb of me to fight and risk tearing the wound open. That being the case, I'll just have to kill you where you stand unless you offer an apology for your bad behavior and call off this nonsense."

"The hell with an apology!" Slocum cried. "You're the one who owes me an apology for not coming right to my office from the train and telling me exactly what you think you're doing in my town."

"All right," Longarm said, forcing a smile. "I was wrong for that and I do apologize. I should have come to meet you straightaway. I didn't, and that was my mistake. On the other hand, you should not have barged into the Hancock Hotel acting like an idiot and insulting me. So now that I've apologized, it's your turn to offer an apology for your boorish behavior this morning."

Brady Slocum spat at the dirt. "There's all the apology you'll get from me, you federal sonofabitch!"

Longarm had heard and seen enough to finally understand that this was not someone he could reason with or even bury the hatchet with, so he took three quick steps forward and smashed Brady Slocum across the face with the barrel of his pistol.

The town marshal's nose broke and blood gushed out like a small waterfall. Slocum staggered backward, and that's when Longarm kicked the man right in the balls. Longarm knocked him out cold with a straight overhand left to the jaw.

Holbrook's town marshal howled and Longarm kicked the man again under the chin. When Brady Slocum went over backward, there was no question about an apology ever coming from his foul mouth or that he would be able to stand, walk or fight for many a day to come.

"Holy hog fat!" the gambler breathed. "You really beat the hell out of him fast!"

"Slocum was in desperate need of a well-taught lesson in humility."

The stable owner tore off his hat and began wringing its brim all over again. "Marshal Slocum is never going to let you get away with what you just done to him. He's going to find a way to even the score, and he won't rest until you're dead!"

"Then he's not long for this world," Longarm said, holstering his gun. "Now would you please saddle that gelding and then ride him around in the corral for a few minutes so that I can have a look at the way that he moves?"

"Why sure!" Polk said, studying the unconscious town lawman. "But . . ."

"Oh," Longarm added. "What is your asking price for the horse?"

"Thirty dollars," Polk managed to say.

"How much did you say?"

Polk wilted under his gaze. "All right, Marshal. Thirty dollars and I'll throw in a saddle, blanket and bridle. You'll be stealing him from me at that price."

Custis glanced at the gambler, who had not taken his eyes off the unconscious Slocum. "How much does Mr. Polk owe you to clear off his gambling debt?"

"Eighteen dollars."

"In that case," Longarm said, "if I buy the horse all debts will have been laid to rest."

"Not that one," the gambler said, pointing down at Marshal Slocum.

"Oh well," Longarm said with a shrug of his broad shoulders. "By the time I return from Monument Valley, perhaps your Marshal Slocum will have gained some wisdom."

"Don't count on it."

Longarm didn't hear the gambler. He was watching the sorrel with a keen and practiced eye. He really liked the animal's size and conformation. The sorrel was about fifteen hands tall and weighed at least a thousand pounds. It had a handsome head and keen, intelligent eyes. The sorrel appeared to Longarm to be an animal with good sense . . . Too bad he couldn't say the same for Holbrook's Marshal Slocum.

Chapter 6

When Longarm returned to the Hancock Hotel, all the guests were sitting in the lobby waiting to hear what had happened between him and Marshal Slocum. Longarm sank down on one of the couches and said, "There's really nothing to talk about."

"What happened?" Miss Allie asked. "Didn't Marshal Slocum show up at Polk's Stable?"

"Oh, he showed up, and I even apologized to your marshal for not visiting his office first thing after I got off the train."

"Then the matter was settled amicably?" one of the guests said with a satisfied smile. "That's sure the best outcome. No sense in having a fight between two lawmen, because then everyone might decide they aren't reasonable and levelheaded men."

"Well," Longarm drawled, "I see your point, but I'm afraid that Marshal Slocum didn't accept my apology and I had no choice but to deal with him."

"You and he got into a fight?" Miss Allie asked. "Why, you don't look any worse for it."

"It was a very short fight," Longarm told them. "I thought it wise not to risk any serious injury by getting into a rough-and-tumble brawl with your marshal, so I settled the issue as quickly as possible."

The gambler came into the lobby. "He pistol-whipped Slocum across the face, busting his nose. Then he kicked him a couple of times and knocked him out colder than an iced codfish."

"You knocked out Brady Slocum?" Miss Allie asked.

"He really gave me no choice. And if I were on the Holbrook City Council, I'd start looking for a new town marshal, because Brady Slocum isn't mentally stable. At least, that's my opinion."

Everyone was quiet for a moment, and then Miss Allie said, "I don't suppose you'd be interested in replacing Marshal Slocum."

"Afraid not," Longarm said. "In the first place, I like being a Federal Marshal and working out of Denver, and in the second place, I probably make considerably more money than you pay your town marshal. Isn't there anyone here who you can think of that would be interested in that job?"

"Not while Slocum is wearing a badge, there isn't." Miss Allie frowned. "Perhaps what you did to Brady Slocum was in his own best interests. And by that I mean taking a beating might have given him a taste of his own medicine and made him a better man."

"There is always that possibility," Longarm replied. "I'm leaving tomorrow morning and riding north. When

I return, if Brady Slocum wants to sit down and talk about how a lawman should carry out his business and act so that he earns respect instead of fear, then I'd be happy to meet with the man."

"I don't think that will be Marshal Slocum's reaction," the gambler said. "To be a successful gambler, you really have to be able to read men . . . and the way I read our town marshal is that he is bad to the bone."

"I agree," another guest said. "What happened this morning is going to make him even more mean and unreasonable."

Longarm glanced at Miss Allie, who said, "I'm afraid I also have to agree with those two opinions. Brady Slocum was bad before now and he'll be even worse after the beating you just gave him."

"In that case, I'd better run the man out of town before I leave," Longarm said. "Otherwise, I've just created a bad situation for you."

"Are you going to forcibly put him on the train?" one of the guests asked.

"Does he have any family here?"

"No," Allie said. "He's a bachelor and has almost no friends."

"Then I'll see that he takes the first train out of Holbrook today," Longarm decided. "Talk to your mayor or whoever pays the man and make sure that Slocum is paid in full for his time here in office. Holbrook needs to be as fair about this as possible in firing the man. Maybe Slocum will make a fresh start somewhere else and see the error in his past ways."

"I doubt that," Allie told him. "Just be careful when

you put him on the train because I think he's perfectly capable of shooting you in the back as the train pulls out of the station."

"Thanks for the warning," Longarm said. "What train comes through next?"

"The eastbound at ten minutes after eleven this morning."

"Then that's the one I'll put Slocum on," Longarm told them. "In the meantime, I was wondering if Fergus Horn has any friends in this town. I'm looking to talk to someone who might know what he's been up to lately."

"When Fergus is in Holbrook he always stops by to see Dan Shelby. Dan is a gunsmith who sells rifles, pistols and knives to both Indians and whites. His shop is located just up the street."

"Then I believe that I'll go and pay him a visit before I collect Brady Slocum and put him on the eastbound," Longarm told everyone. "But first I need to go up to my room and change my bandage."

"Do you need any fresh bandaging or tape?" Miss Allie asked.

"As a matter of fact, I do," Longarm told her.

"I'll get some and be right up to your room," she offered.

"Much obliged, Miss Allie."

Longarm went up to his room and took off his coat, vest, string tie and shirt. He had been in such a hurry this morning to get down to breakfast on time that he had not changed his bandages. Standing in front of a little mirror and looking at the stitches that Molly Malloy had put in his side to close up the knife wound, he thought that he ought to sit down and write her a brief note just to say that he'd arrived safely in Holbrook, Arizona Territory. No need to explain the trouble he'd just had with the town marshal. He'd try to remember to buy her a nice piece of polished petrified wood as a little gift upon his return.

"Marshal, are you decent?" came Miss Allie's voice from the hallway. "I've got some clean bandaging for you."

"Come on in, but I have to confess that I'm not always 'decent' around someone as pretty as yourself, Miss Allie."

She laughed and came inside. "My land!" she exclaimed. "You've got more scars on your body than cards in a full deck."

"Not quite," he told her. "But I've been in quite a few bad scrapes. I heal quickly, though."

"Let me see that wound you've got stitched up," she said, placing the bandages down on the bed and coming over to inspect his side. "Kinda sloppy work for a doctor, I'd have to say."

"A doctor didn't do the stitching," Longarm told her. "It was done by a friend of mine because I was in a big hurry to catch the train out of Denver."

"Well, he must have been in a hurry as well."

"It wasn't a he. It was a she."

"Oh, I see. You have a lady friend and I'll just bet that you've set a wedding date, too."

"Miss Malloy would like to set a date, but I'm resisting," he told her. "I'd make the worst kind of husband, but Molly stubbornly refuses to accept that."

"Some women are blind when it comes to a tall, handsome man with some breeding."

"Is that how you see me?"

"It is," Miss Allie told him. "Now let me clean this up a bit because it is oozing. Then I'll put a fresh bandage on it and you'll be all fixed up and ready to face Brady Slocum. You can put him on the train and get that bad apple out of our lives forever."

"You sound as if you really dislike your marshal."

"In the worst way," she told him. "I campaigned hard against him but he ran off his only challenger and so there was no alternative but to hire Slocum. I warned the town council that he would be a terrible mistake but they ignored me and now we're all paying for it."

"No longer," he assured her. "The man is going to get a one-way ticket on the eastbound train."

Miss Allie smiled. "I'm grateful to you for that. I wish that you were staying here a few days longer."

"I've got a job to do, and the sooner I get up to Monument Valley and find out what Fergus Horn is up to and what is going on with his wife, the sooner I'll be finished."

"I hope she's all right. I don't think that such a woman should be up in that hard country, and certainly not with a husband like Fergus Horn. The man is not to be trusted."

"So I've heard," Longarm told her as he dressed and then strapped on his gun belt. "Well, I'm going to talk to your gunsmith and then go find Slocum and tell him that he's on his way out of town."

"Just be careful," Miss Allie warned. "Because I can't even imagine the terrible rage that is boiling in his twisting guts."

"I'll be *very* careful," Longarm promised as he headed

out the door and down the hallway to the stairs leading into the lobby.

Longarm was halfway down the stairs when he sensed something was wrong in the hotel lobby. At the bend in the stair's landing he paused and then realized that the hotel's guests were wearing expressions of fear.

Longarm immediately saw the reason for the fear. Marshal Brady Slocum, face battered and swollen almost beyond recognition, was aiming a double-barreled shotgun and gazing up at him.

Longarm jumped sideways just as the twin blasts shattered the stillness of the lobby and tore the stair railing into a million splinters. He felt as if needles were plunging through every pore of his body, and then he collapsed into a swirling pit of darkness.

Chapter 7

Longarm awoke with a painful start. He looked around and recognized nothing except Miss Allie, who was standing beside a tall, thin, dark-complexioned man with shoulder-length black hair.

"Where am I?"

"You're in my room," Miss Allie said, leaning in close. "It's a miracle that you weren't killed in that shotgun blast, but you were just splintered in a few places by pieces of the stair railing, and then you fell off the landing and hit your head on a wooden table."

Longarm nodded as he began to remember what had happened. "What about Brady Slocum?"

"The gambler pulled a pistol and shot him, but Slocum managed to draw his own gun and kill Mr. Smith. He then rode out of town on that sorrel horse that you bought at Polk's Stable."

Longarm swore under his breath. "Do you have any idea where Slocum might have gone?"

"He rode straight north," the dark-complexioned man said. "He's heading into the Navajo Reservation."

Longarm raised his hand and wiped his face. "How long have I been unconscious?"

"Just one day. You really hit your head hard on that table downstairs. Smashed it to pieces."

"Better the table than my skull," Longarm said dryly. "I'll pay you for all the damages."

"We're just glad that you survived the shotgun blasts and the fall," Miss Allie told him. "We talked about it downstairs and figured that the reason Brady Slocum missed so badly is that his eyes were swollen almost shut from the beating you gave him at the stables. The only reason he was able to kill the gambler is that Mr. Smith's gun misfired. When that happened, Slocum stepped right up to him and shot him three times in the belly."

Her voice caught in her throat. "I'm afraid that Mr. Smith died . . . very hard."

Longarm tried to sit up but the world started to spin. "Oh," he groaned, "I'm not quite ready to go on a manhunt."

"You have a concussion," the man said. "Oh, my name is Ira."

"I figured that's who you were. Did Miss Allie tell you that I need a guide to go find both Fergus Horn and his wife . . . or rather former wife . . . the beautiful Veronica Sutton?"

"Yes. I can find Horn but I don't know where his woman is now."

"Have you even seen or heard of her lately?"

"No," Ira said. "I think she is either long gone or else she is probably dead. That woman was known very well among my people and she was respected for her kindness."

"I wonder how long it's been since anyone has seen her," Longarm mused. "That's the question I'd like to ask when we get up around Monument Valley."

Ira simply shrugged his shoulders. "Maybe tomorrow we can ride."

"I'll have to find me another horse to buy. That will leave me pretty short of funds."

"I will find you a good horse cheap. Later, when we kill Slocum, then you will have two horses and can sell one for money."

"I'll try to arrest the man," Longarm said. "But after what he's done, I'm sure he knows that he'll face the hangman and will fight to the death."

"Maybe Navajo kill him before we can," Ira suggested. "Slocum is a bad man. Hurt many drunken Navajo, jail many who committed no crimes. Much hated on the reservation by everyone."

"If that is true," Longarm said, "then why would he go up there in the first place?"

"Maybe only go a little ways north, then turn east or west to throw off anyone who would dare to follow."

"Yes," Longarm said, "that makes sense. At any rate, I'm going to have to hunt the man down and I sure could use your help."

"I'll help."

"Thanks. I hope to leave tomorrow."

"You may have to rest for a few days."

"We'll see," Longarm told the half-breed. "But, Ira, you'd better understand that I can't pay you much money."

"I'll take my pay in trade with the horses and saddles

when we're done . . . including that sorrel gelding. We talk about it later."

"Fair enough," Longarm said. "My wallet was in my coat pocket. I think I've got maybe twenty dollars left in it, so take all of the money and buy that cheap horse and whatever else we will need to first go after Brady Slocum and then head on up to Monument Valley and see if we can find Fergus Horn."

"I'll do that," Ira said, picking up Longarm's coat, which was torn and spattered with blood. He picked out the wallet, took all the money and put the empty wallet back in the coat. "You're a lucky, lucky man, Marshal Long. Not many men get in the way of two shotgun shells and live to fight again with only a cracked head."

"I know I'm lucky, Ira. I just wish that poor Mr. Smith hadn't been shot to death. Most gamblers I know haven't a lot of decency in them . . . but that one sure as hell did."

Ira left the room. Longarm's head was throbbing, so he eased it back down on the pillow and closed his eyes. "Things haven't gotten off to a very good start for me in your town of Holbrook, Miss Allie."

"It's a hard place and it demands much of us all," she said. "But Holbrook is also a good railroad town with a lot of decent folks just trying to make ends meet. I hope you don't think badly of us."

"Of course not," he said. "I just wish that things would have gone a lot smoother since I climbed down from the train. I kind of feel like I've really made a botch of things since I arrived."

"No, you haven't," she argued. "We had a hell of a

problem with Marshal Brady Slocum. Everyone knew that he needed to be fired, but given his temper and how dangerous he is, no one had the guts to step forward and tell him to leave his badge on his desk and get out of Holbrook. You've solved our problem by driving him away, and it's not your fault that a pistol jammed and he murdered poor Mr. Smith."

"Thanks for saying that, but I feel responsible for the man's death, and even though I'm here to find out about Fergus Horn and his wife, you can bet that I won't leave this country until Slocum is brought to justice."

"I hope you or Ira kill him," Allie said, bitterness in her voice. "That would be the best thing to do and it would be justified."

"I'm sure you're right and that's most likely what will happen," Longarm replied. "What can you tell me about Ira?"

"He's a half-breed who was raised at a trading post up on the reservation. He's had some schooling, so he can read and write. He's also a healer and a pretty important person among the members of his family. I have seen the man's wife. Betty is a good woman from an important family. They have a large family but Ira is restless and is often gone hunting or making medicine among The People. I don't really know anything more about the man except that he is said to be an expert shot."

"That's all that I need to know about him," Longarm said, a hammer pounding inside his head. "A man has a right to be left to his own private thoughts and ways."

"I think so, too," Allie told him. "But I can tell you this . . . I'd trust my life with Ira."

"Well, I may have to do that," Longarm told her. "Given the way things have gotten off to such a bad start, it's hard to imagine them suddenly getting easy."

"You rest and I'll bring up some food after supper. Tonight we're having fried chicken and hot dumplings. Are you hungry?"

"I can't say that I am," Longarm admitted, "but I'd better force myself to eat or I'll get weak."

"That's right," Allie agreed. "And when you've tasted the chicken and dumplings, I'm sure that you'll still want a big slice of apple pie."

Longarm managed to smile. "I'm sure you're right."

She patted him on the leg and her hand slid up to rest on his thigh. "After we got you up here and onto the bed and I shooed everyone out, I undressed you."

He lifted the sheet and saw that he was stark naked. "I can see that."

"You're hanging pretty long down there, Marshal. To put it frankly, you're downright impressive."

"You think so?"

"Oh, honey, I *know* so." Allie kissed his cheek. "I'm a few years older than you, but I've still got a lively bounce."

"Doesn't surprise me a bit," he said. "You hinting at something more than good food and apple pie?"

"I just might be," she said with a wink as her fingers traced their way up his thigh. "After all, you *are* in my bed."

"Yeah," he chuckled, "I guess I am at that."

"Take a nap and get ready for that supper and dessert," she ordered. "Maybe *two* desserts, if you're up to it."

"We'll see, Miss Allie. We'll just have to wait until tonight and see."

* * *

Later that night, when all her hotel guests had gone either to bed or were out at the saloons to drink, Allie sent the kitchen help home and dimmed the lobby lights. When she climbed the shattered staircase, she marveled at how anyone could have stood upon it and survived. It would cost at least a hundred dollars to hire a professional woodworker to come and rebuild the stairs, but Allie wasn't all that concerned with the expense.

Mostly, she was just glad to be rid of Marshal Brady Slocum, who had abused the whores that she allowed to come up into her hotel rooms when requested by a customer. And once, Slocum had even dared to break through her door and rape her repeatedly.

She tried to have the man killed by offering a bounty on Marshal Slocum's head, but the man had found out about it and then beaten her so badly that she'd been unable to leave her room for almost two weeks.

Now, Brady Slocum was the one whose face was a misshapen mass of purple and black, and who was on the run for his life. And as she stepped around all the damage on the stairs and moved up to her room to sleep with Marshal Custis Long, Allie felt as if a great weight had suddenly been lifted from her shoulders.

"Ira or Custis Long will kill that ornery sonofabitch," she said to herself with real satisfaction. "And if they bring Slocum's bullet-riddled body back to Holbrook for burial, I'm going to pay the undertaker to take a short walk while I lift my skirt, squat and piss on Slocum's corpse!"

Chapter 8

Longarm was on top of Miss Allie, giving her all that he had left after already taking her twice since midnight. When he groaned and unleashed his diminished torrent of seed, the woman shuddered with satisfaction and lay breathing heavily.

"I can't take any more of you tonight," Miss Allie confessed. "I feel like you've about split me in half."

He rolled off of her and said, "I'm sorry if I hurt you."

"Oh, I'll recover," she assured him as he lay staring out the window at the fading light of the stars.

"What are you thinking about?" Miss Allie asked, looking at the dark silhouette of his face. "Are you feeling guilty because of that woman that's waiting for you back in Denver?"

"No," he answered. "Molly knows that I am not faithful, and I never expected her to be faithful to me."

"No commitment, huh?"

"That's right," he answered. "But when I'm in Denver, I don't mess with other women. I treat Molly with respect and she gives me the same."

"And she's happy with that arrangement?"

"I don't know."

"I'm pretty sure that she isn't," Miss Allie said. "A woman likes a man who is not screwing other women when he is off someplace or when the opportunity arises."

"I suppose that's true, but Molly and I understand each other pretty well and we get along with the arrangement that we've made."

"I'm worried about you leaving and going up on the reservation," Miss Allie said. "Those people really don't like federal officers. There are outlaws hiding up there in Monument Valley. Men who have killed men and who are wanted by the law."

"I can handle it," Longarm said. "And I have Ira to steer us through the worst of things."

"Ira can be trusted with your life," Miss Allie said. "But I'm sure he has his share of enemies up on the reservation. Some of them would like him dead, and they sure wouldn't mind taking a federal marshal along as a prize."

"Nothing in life is dead safe," Longarm said. "And I'm not a fool like Brady Slocum. I don't push my weight around and I don't even show my badge unless it's necessary."

"I'll be looking for you when you return," she said, kissing his cheek. "Now let's get us a few hours of shut-eye."

"I could use it," he admitted, rolling over onto his back and falling asleep instantly.

* * *

Longarm slept late and when he awoke the sun was high and he felt like a new man. The night before he and Miss Allie had coupled three times. He should have been exhausted, but he wasn't.

Longarm climbed out of bed slowly, and when his head didn't begin to spin or pound he dressed and looked at the clock on Allie's dresser. "Ten-fifteen," he said to himself. "I've missed breakfast completely."

His gun was hanging on the bedpost and there was a note on the dresser from Miss Allie that explained how she had gone to her usual women's knitting group and might not be around when he came down to the lobby or even when he left town with Ira.

Longarm understood that Miss Allie was probably a little worried that, in the cold light of day, he might see that she had some wrinkles on her face and suddenly find her unattractive. Of course, that would not have been the case, but he understood that she was a little self-conscious about being five or ten years his senior.

Longarm went next door to his own room and packed his bag, making sure that he had what was needed for the journey north. A few minutes later when he descended the stairs there were two hotel guests reading papers in the lobby and they both greeted him warmly.

"Marshal, we sure are glad that you came out of this alive," an older guest named Pinkston said. "It's a miracle that you're still among the living."

"You're plenty right about that, Mr. Pinkston. I'm just sorry that Mr. Smith was shot dead."

"He suffered greatly," Pinkston replied, his head and jowls shivering with outrage. "I've never seen anything

so cold-blooded. Slocum could have just hit him with
his gun or his fist. As you well know, Mr. Smith wasn't a
large or strong man, and he'd have been down and out
with just one punch! But Slocum seemed to take delight
in putting lead into the poor man's stomach."

"I'll see that he pays for that," Longarm promised.
"In spades."

"Glad to hear it, Marshal," Pinkston said. "Make Brady
Slocum die real slow and in agonizing pain, like Mr.
Smith."

Longarm nodded and left the hotel. He looked up and
down the street, really hoping to see Miss Allie, but he
wasn't surprised that she wasn't to be seen. Not sure
where to find Ira, he headed toward Polk's Stable, but
the half-breed seemed to appear from nowhere.

"I've got our horses saddled and packed," Ira said.
"This way."

"How did you know I'd be physically up for the trip
today?"

"Miss Allie told me on her way to her knitting cir-
cle."

"Of course," Longarm said. "I didn't get a chance to
tell her good-bye."

Ira started to smile and say something, but he changed
his mind and just nodded.

Their horses were tied behind a small house at the
edge of town and Ira had bought all the supplies they'd
need. Ira was riding a pinto and Longarm's horse was a
tall dapple gray gelding with a rather large head.

"The gray is a good animal," Ira said. "He's tough
and fast."

"But not as fast as your pinto pony, I'll bet."

Ira just shrugged. "You're a big man and you need a big horse to carry you far. That one belonged to one of my cousins and he'll buy him back from you for fifteen dollars."

"Well," Longarm said, "assuming I get everything done that I'm hoping to do, then I'll be boarding the eastbound train and I sure won't be taking this horse back to Colorado. And I see that you've got us a couple of repeating rifles."

Longarm pulled a Winchester out of his saddle boot and worked the lever. It had a smooth action but the rifle itself appeared to have been used hard. Its stock was cracked and wrapped in deerskin that was tacked down tight.

"Is this one accurate?"

"You'll figure it out after we get out in the brush," Ira said. "Shoots a little to the right but still accurate, if you know how much it's off your aim."

"Your rifle doesn't look a whole lot better than this one."

"It'll do," Ira said. "It always fires, and I don't miss what I aim for."

"I'll bet not."

Ira tightened his cinch then he swung up into his saddle and waited for Longarm to mount the gray.

"Before we leave Holbrook," Longarm told the halfbreed, "I want to stop and have a word with Dan Shelby, who owns the gunsmith shop. I'm told he's a friend of Fergus Horn and perhaps he can tell me a few things about the man."

"He'll tell you nothing," Ira said.

"Why is that?"

"Shelby and Horn are two of a kind. Not good men."

Longarm nodded. "Well, I'll talk to the man anyway before we leave. It never hurts to try. Shelby might know where we can find Horn and what he's up to these days."

In reply, Ira simply kicked his pony into a trot and headed up the street. Longarm mounted the gray and trotted after the man, and when he came abreast of the gunsmith shop, he reined up and dismounted.

"I take it you're not coming in with me," Longarm said.

"Shelby doesn't like me and I don't like Shelby," Ira replied. "Better I stay out here and wait."

"Suit yourself."

Longarm went into the gun shop and stood back while an ordinary man in his forties sold a customer a box of bullets and tried to sell him an eight-gauge shotgun for ten dollars. When the transaction was completed and the customer had departed, Longarm stepped up to the counter and said, "I'm Marshal Custis Long from Denver."

"I know who you are," Shelby said, ignoring Longarm's outstretched hand and trying to look mean. "And I've got nothing to say to you about anyone or anything."

"Not a very cooperative attitude," Longarm said, dropping his hand to his side. "I was hoping that you could tell me where to find Fergus Horn and even what he's up to these days."

"I don't know a thing about Fergus Horn," Shelby said, "other than that he lives way up near Monument Valley and runs a little trading post. That's all that I can tell you."

"Oh," Longarm drawled, "I very much doubt that's true. I was listening to you tell that customer about the eight-gauge double-barreled shotgun. I might be willing to buy it for ten dollars. Can I have a look at the gun?"

"You know what?" Shelby said after a long pause, "I just decided that the shotgun really isn't for sale."

"How's that?"

"Well, I'm kinda picky about who I sell weapons to, and I just don't think that I want to sell the shotgun to you."

Longarm felt his cheeks burn, and since the shotgun was lying on a nearby table he just went over and picked it up. "It's old but it sure would blow the hell out of whatever you aimed it at," he said, breaking the gun and turning the barrels to the window so that he could see if they were clean and not pitted. "Tell you what, Shelby, I'll buy it and a few shells."

"Not for sale."

"Oh yes, it is," Longarm told the man, jamming the empty gun into Shelby's chest hard enough to knock him back against the wall. "Now give me a half dozen shells for this beast and I'll give you an extra dollar for the ammunition."

It was Dan Shelby's turn to flush with anger, and he even started to say something, but when Longarm shoved the barrels in under his chin and smiled, Shelby nodded. even though they both knew the shotgun wasn't loaded.

"Marshal, I hope that old shotgun blows up in your face," Shelby hissed as Longarm made his purchase. "And it just might."

"I don't think so," Longarm said, dropping the shotgun shells into his coat pocket. "But it just might save my life if I get into a bad fix. Have a good day, Mr. Shelby."

"Go to hell!"

"Maybe I will," Longarm said. passing out the door and untying his horse.

Ira took in the big-barreled shotgun with a glance. "I'm surprised that Shelby would sell that thing to you."

"He needed a little encouragement," Longarm said. "But I can be pretty persuasive when I want something badly enough."

"Yeah, I'll just bet you can at that," Ira said, the hint of a smile at the corner of his mouth. "Let's ride, Marshal. We got a long way to go."

"How far?"

"Hundred miles or more of tough country. Take us three days to get up to the top of the reservation."

"Do you know where we can find Fergus Horn?"

"I know where he used to be," Ira said. "Don't know if he'll be there anymore or not."

"Only one way to find out," Longarm said as they rode up the middle of the main street then turned their horses to the north and set them to an easy canter. Longarm liked the way that the gray gelding moved, but he didn't like dark clouds that were gathering just up ahead.

Two hours later the wind began to howl and it started to rain. "Looks like we're riding into a bad thunderstorm!"

"Yeah! You can tell it rained hard up here yesterday and it's probably gonna be even worse today." Ira leaned out of his saddle and pointed to the wet, red earth. "I lost Brady Slocum's tracks about five miles back."

"Maybe we can pick them up again tomorrow."

"Maybe," the half-breed said, but he didn't sound too optimistic. "But I doubt it. This is slick-rock country up ahead, and a horse doesn't leave much of a track even when the ground is dry. But when the rain hits the red rock, it washes everything away."

"You think that Slocum might be heading for Monument Valley?"

"Only if he wants to ambush and kill you," Ira replied. "And from what I've heard about the man, that's likely."

"Or he might have circled back to Holbrook, hoping to shoot me from a rooftop."

"Could be," Ira agreed. "I guess you won't know until a bullet comes your way, huh, Marshal?"

"I'd sure as hell rather have some warning," Longarm shouted into the wind.

"I can tell you this much. Brady Slocum won't rest until either you or he is dead."

Longarm pulled the brim of his hat down tight. and up ahead he saw a bolt of lightning shiver down to strike a big juniper pine. The treetop exploded and then began to smoke in the driving rain. A moment later, it burst into flames. The gray gelding shied and snorted in fear, and they gave the burning tree a wide berth.

"Bad sign!" Ira called. "Real bad!"

Longarm didn't have a reply. Most Indians saw signs and read deep meanings in things like lightning and a lame coyote crossing their path or a burning tree, but as far as he was concerned, it was all just native superstition.

Chapter 9

Longarm had experienced a few Southwest storms in his time, but this was one of the worst. The wind was howling, the sky was boiling with dark clouds and the rain was slanting directly into their faces as they tried to make their way north.

"Hey!" Longarm shouted. "You know this country. We need to hole up for the night and wait out this storm!"

"I thought you were in a big hurry to get to Monument Valley and see what that damned Fergus Horn is up to."

"I already know what he's up to, and it's causing big trouble!" Longarm yelled. "And I need to find out what happened to his wife!"

Before Ira could shoot back a reply, another bolt of lightning lanced out of the sky and struck a rock pinnacle not a quarter mile away. The gray gelding whirled in panic and tried to run. Longarm was hauling back on the reins when the horse tumbled down into a deep and brush-choked arroyo. He kicked free of his stirrups, struck the muddy ground hard and rolled through a pile of tumbleweeds until he came to a stop against a boulder.

Ira's pinto was rearing and pulling at the reins and he had to calm the animal down before he could help Longarm. "You all right, Marshal? You sure took a hard fall. This damned arroyo was almost covered up with sage and brush, and I doubt that the gray even saw it until it was too late."

"If I find him I'll shoot the loco sonofabitch!" Longarm spat, slapping red mud from his face.

"That wouldn't be a very good idea unless you'd like to walk all the way back to Holbrook and buy another horse."

Longarm cussed and fought back the pain. "I'll bet those damn stitches in my side broke free and the wound opened up again."

"Can you stand?" Ira asked, extending a hand.

Longarm took the half-breed's outstretched hand and hauled himself erect. "My horse is gone!" he shouted into the storm.

"If you're okay to stay here a few minutes, I'll ride after that horse," Ira said. "It probably didn't go very far."

Longarm was doubled up with pain and his head was throbbing. His clothes were covered with red mud and he was standing in a cold, driving rain. "I'll be all right. Get the damned horse and let's find some shelter if there's any to be had nearby."

"I know just the place," Ira shouted as he leaped back onto his pinto and went galloping off to find the gray gelding.

Longarm sat down on a rock and bent over as the rain kept beating against him. He'd lost his hat someplace, and at the moment he was hurting too much to go and search for the damned thing. Maybe Ira had been right when he'd said that the burning juniper was a bad sign and there might be bad things coming at them in the next few days.

But right now, Longarm knew he would have traded most everything he owned for a roof over his head, a fire at his feet and a bottle of good whiskey to sip while this miserable storm raged directly overhead.

After a few minutes Longarm pushed himself to his feet, gritting his teeth against the pain. He was bleeding but knew he wasn't going to bleed to death. He walked around in the arroyo and finally located his mud-stained Stetson. He was about to sit down and rest again when he heard a roaring sound like that of a distant onrushing train.

Flash flood!

Longarm threw himself at the steep bank, clawing for footing, grabbing bushes and hauling himself upward in a wild scramble for his life. He wasn't a moment too quick reaching the top of the bank, because a churning wave of tumbleweeds, brush and all kinds of matter came hurling down the arroyo, sweeping away everything in its foaming path.

Longarm collapsed in exhaustion at the top of the arroyo. After only a few minutes, the roar subsided and the water suddenly lost its force and became just a tumbling stream of muddy water and flotsam.

An exceedingly miserable hour passed before Ira returned with both horses. The rain was still pelting down in cold sheets, and Longarm managed to haul himself back into his saddle.

"This way!" Ira shouted. "It's not far."

Longarm ducked his head and let the gelding follow Ira's pinto. It seemed like they traveled for at least two hours before they suddenly came to a stop before Navajo hogan. Longarm had never been inside of a Navajo hogan, but he would have stepped into a grizzly bear's den to get out of this cold wind and rain.

"Where do I tie my horse?" he yelled into the storm.

"Just wrap your reins around your saddle horn and grab your bag and our weapons," Ira shouted. "These horses will be taken care of by the boys."

Longarm didn't argue. He untied his canvas bag, grabbed the double-barreled shotgun and the old Winchester rifle that belonged to Ira and followed the man inside the big hogan.

It was surprisingly warm inside, and well lit inside despite the fact that there were no windows. The doorway was covered with the tanned hide of a bay horse on the outside and the hides of shorn sheep sewn together on the inside, making a heavy double flap able to withstand the outside elements. Longarm glanced around and saw at least seven or eight family members sitting on beautifully woven Navajo rugs and sheepskins around a crackling cooking and heating fire. There was a pot of corn and bean stew with chunks of mutton bubbling over the coals. The women of the hogan ranged from an old grandma to a young and pretty girl of about sixteen. They were dressed in long, colorful velvet skirts. An old

.

man smoked a pipe near the fire, and several children stared at Longarm with round, black eyes.

One of the women, who looked to be in her late thirties, got up from her place by the fire and came forward to bow slightly to Longarm. "Welcome to our home."

"Thank you," Longarm said, removing his mud-caked hat.

"Ira," the woman said, turning, "I did not expect you to bring a white man here as your guest, but he is welcome."

"This man is hurt. I will make medicine for him before he gets weak and sick. He is hungry and so am I."

"It is a bad day to be outside," she said to Longarm with a warm smile. "My name is Betty. This is my home and these people are my family."

"I am honored to meet all of you," Longarm said. "And sorry that I am such a mess and in a bit of difficulty."

"It is good you are here," Betty told him. "Please sit by the fire and warm yourself while we get something for you to eat."

Longarm's coat and hat were taken, as well as his gun, soggy vest and shirt. He sat bare-chested on a Navajo rug by the fire and was fed corn, bean and mutton stew. It was hot and spicy with sage and other herbs, and it was delicious. Longarm ate three bowls of the stew and the children tittered with ill-concealed laughter at his ravenous appetite. Later, his wound was cleaned and then a warm poultice was applied and he lay down to rest. The last thing Longarm heard was the laughter of women and children, the low talking of the Navajo and the booming of thunder over the vast reservation.

                              *   *   *

When Longarm awoke he was staring up at the faces of
three small children who seemed very curious about his
drooping handlebar mustache. They jumped back when
his eyes popped open, and when he sat up they scurried
outside.

With the hide flap thrown back, the sun was now
streaming into the hogan from the east so that Longarm
knew it was morning and the violent storm had passed.
He heard the sounds of people talking in Navajo outside,
and when he climbed to his feet Betty appeared to touch
his forehead.

"You have no more fever and the wound is not so red
and mean looking as it was yesterday. Do you feel better?"

"Much better. Thank you for your hospitality and that
great stew."

"You are welcome. My husband tells me that you had
trouble in Holbrook with Marshal Brady Slocum."

"Yes. He tried to kill me, and it was necessary that I
hurt him."

"He is too proud, that one. And mean, too! You must
be careful. And the elders think you have come because
of that other bad white man . . . Mr. Fergus Horn."

"They are right," Longarm admitted. "I hear that he is
making a lot of trouble and trying to cause an uprising
among your people."

"That is true," she said. "He has talked against the
United States government and he is telling The People
that the army horse soldiers will come again and round
us all up and send us on another Long Walk to Fort
Defiance in the New Mexico Territory."

"Horn is lying to your people."

Betty shrugged her shoulders. "I believe you, but some believe Horn and are very worried. The young men especially are ready to fight and die if the soldiers come to take them and their families away. Last time, so many died that the crying has not yet stopped among The People."

"I am here to assure the Navajo that Fergus Horn is a liar and that I will stop him from telling so many bad lies. But first, I must find him, and I also hope to find his wife."

Betty shrugged. "She has not been seen for a long time. I do not know if she is alive anymore."

"It is said that Fergus Horn has found gold and silver. Do you know if this is true?"

For a moment, Betty was silent with eyes lowered, and then she raised her chin and said, "I only know that Fergus Horn has much money and he pays women to wait on him like slaves and do all that he asks. He also has a trading post and many guns and men who are bad."

"Why don't The People make him leave their reservation?"

"Because he is part Navajo and has much power." She looked away and saw Ira braiding a rawhide lariat out by some flat red rocks. "Do not let him kill my husband."

"I won't."

"Or let Slocum kill him, either."

"I'll do my best to keep both Ira and myself alive."

"My husband says that he saw many troubling signs since leaving Holbrook. Maybe you should just go back to the place where you live."

"I would like to do that but I cannot," Longarm told

her. "And besides, if Fergus Horn is stirring up your people to fight, then I need to stop the man before the soldiers come to fight. If that happens, blood will flow like water on your reservation."

"I know," Betty said quietly. "But what you do with Slocum and Fergus Horn is *your* business. My business is to see that I have a happy husband and that my children can watch their father grow old."

"You could tell Ira not to go with me up to Monument Valley. If he chose not to go, I would understand that after having seen your family and this good life."

"Ira would go even if I asked him to stay here. Ira does what he wants and he is a good husband and man. But he is troubled by recent signs and omens, and so am I."

"I will send him back to you if it looks like I am going to be killed," Longarm promised her. "That is all that I can do."

"It is good that we now have an understanding," Betty told him while looking straight into his eyes. "You must wait one more day in order to be strong enough to ride to Monument Valley.

"I'm sure that you're right," Longarm told her as a boy on a small bay pony came riding over a hill driving a small flock of sheep along with a few Angora goats. "Thank you for your hospitality. One more night, then tomorrow we leave."

"Yes," Betty agreed. "One more night with food, medicine and rest."

Chapter 10

Former Holbrook town marshal Brady Slocum had weathered the fierce storm by huddling under a rock with his rain slicker pulled tight over his head. During the night, his horse had galloped away in fear, and now that the storm had passed, Slocum was wet, miserable and blaming all of his misfortune on United States Marshal Custis Long.

Until Custis Long's unexpected arrival, Brady Slocum had thought his life was going to be easy, satisfying and prosperous. He had forged his will over the Holbrook townspeople and they had paid him his asking price out of raw fear. Now, however, he was no longer held in fear or respect, and it was all on account of the damned federal marshal.

Hungry, soaked, miserable and angry, Brady Slocum was a man on a mission, and that mission was simply to find Custis Long and kill him any way he could. And if the half-breed, Ira, didn't like it, then Slocum was plenty

happy to send Ira to the Happy Hunting Grounds . . . if
the Navajo believed in that place. Or maybe hell . . . it
just didn't matter.

When the sun was full up over the eastern horizon
and the storm was clearly past him, Slocum pushed himself to his feet and walked through the heavy, clinging
mud in the direction of Ira's hogan. His horse had almost assuredly headed back to Holbrook, and he'd claim
the beast later. Right now, however, the nearest place
that he knew he could find food and shelter was Ira's
hogan. He had never actually been to that hogan, but he
was pretty sure that it wouldn't be difficult to find if he
didn't go lame first.

All day long Brady Slocum trudged through the red
clay mud, and just before sunset he finally saw a lazy
plume of smoke rising from a Navajo hogan. His feet
were killing him and he knew that they were covered
with blisters. Slocum's belly rumbled from hunger and
he was bone weary after the nearly twenty-mile hike.
But here he was at last.

Slocum sat down on a rock with his back to the low-
ering sun and studied Ira's home with great interest. The
first thing he was looking for was Ira's pinto pony and
the horse that the federal marshal would have ridden in
order to get here. With a smile on his lips, Slocum saw
both animals penned in a flimsy pole corral that also held
sheep and goats.

"Good!" Slocum hissed. "I'll wait until after they're
all asleep and then I'll give them the wake-up call of
their damned lives."

*　　*　　*

It was a hard wait. Slocum was so hungry he could have eaten an entire burro, and he was chilled the moment the sun set in the west. But he was a patient man and the prize was worth the pain, so he chewed on a stick, checked his guns and waited as darkness deepened over the vast and empty landscape. And all the time he waited, he saw only a few people come and go from the hogan; all of them went into the brush to probably take their evening shit.

Once, just faintly, he saw the outline of a big man, and Slocum would have bet his bottom dollar that it was the federal marshal. He raised his rifle and took aim but reluctantly lowered the weapon knowing that in the poor light the odds of killing Custis Long were not in his favor.

And also there was the half-breed, Ira. Brady Slocum knew that Ira was a man to be reckoned with, both among the Navajo and the whites. Ira was known to be a crack shot and an outstanding tracker.

Yes, Brady Slocum told himself, *I could probably kill the federal marshal, but then Ira would have the advantage on me, knowing the land and having the support of his family to go against me.*

So Slocum dropped his rifle across his cold and rain-soaked pants, bowed his weary head and waited for the moon to rise and light up the night. He did not have a pocket watch but he felt pretty confident that he could judge when it became midnight.

"I'll have to kill them early tomorrow morning," he said finally reaching a decision that he did not like. "Wait until they come outside and then shoot them down like a pair of dogs."

*   *   *

Slocum slept fitfully that night, and in the morning he awoke feeling sick from the night's bitter cold and the severe hardship of the previous day's long walk. Slocum placed the back of his hand against his forehead and discovered that he was running a temperature. His body shook with chills and he cursed at his physical failings. The very last thing in the world he needed today was to become ill and therefore unable to ambush the marshal and the half-breed.

Only when Slocum looked closely did he realize that two horses were missing from the corral, proving that the men he sought to kill had saddled earlier and left. Brady Slocum glanced up at the sun and knew at once that it was mid-morning and that, because of his fever and exhaustion, he had overslept.

A boy left the hogan and went to the corral. He opened the pole corral and drove out the sheep and goats. The boy had a dog with him, and together they pushed the bleating sheep and goats out of the pen and herded them off toward some distant pasture.

Slocum watched the kid and his dog disappear over a hill and decided that he had no choice but to hike down to the hogan and get help. To his dismay, he found it difficult to climb to his feet and start moving. Every muscle in his body protested with pain and his feet were a mass of blisters. But no one saw him approach, and when he opened the hogan's door flap and looked inside, he saw Ira's family.

"What are you doing here!" Betty cried, jumping to her feet.

"I'm out for a little stroll," Slocum replied with sarcasm. "And I got hungry and tired. I want food and I want it now."

"I give you nothing!" Betty hissed, trying to position herself in front of her children. "Get out of my house!"

Slocum levered a shell into the rifle and pointed it at the oldest girl in the hogan. "You'll feed and take care of me until I'm ready to leave or I'll kill every damn one of you, starting with your oldest daughter."

Betty looked into his eyes and saw that this man would do exactly as he threatened. They were the eyes of a hungry coyote capable of ripping out the throats of sheep or goats without hesitation or regret.

"Sit down and I will feed you mutton stew," she said.

"Glad to hear that you're going to be smart about this," Slocum told her.

"But if you hurt or kill any of my children, then I will kill you," Betty warned.

"Well, at least we have an understanding about the killing part," he told her.

"And if you kill me before I can kill you," Betty added, "then my husband will hunt you down and kill you slow."

Brady Slocum felt weak with hunger and exhaustion. "Enough talk," he snarled, nearly falling onto a blanket placed near the family's small cooking fire.

"How long will you stay?"

"I don't know," he confessed. "Your husband and that federal marshal musta lit out of here not long after daybreak this morning. They're headed for Monument Valley, ain't they?"

Betty said nothing.

"All right," Slocum said wearily. "We'll be like a big

happy family until I decide I'm strong enough to leave. Until then all you have to do is to obey my commands. Do that and none of you get hurt or killed. But, if you try to get clever, then I'll kill every last one of you."

Betty went outside for firewood. When her children started to follow, Slocum said, "Whoa up there, kids! You're all staying put. I like to look at your happy faces."

The Navajo children just stared at him. Slocum knew that they were afraid, but to their credit they did not exhibit fear.

"So how old are you?" he asked, pointing to the oldest girl.

She didn't answer and he wondered if she even knew English or if she just detested him too much to speak.

"I am ten," the oldest boy finally offered. "And I do not like you and neither does my mother and father."

"Well!" Slocum said. "Ain't that a crying damn shame! Sure makes me feel terrible. Do you know what I'm going to do?"

The boy shook his head.

"Well," Slocum said, "as soon as I'm feeling a little better, I'm going to climb on one of your ugly damned ponies and ride north after the federal marshal and your father. And then do you know what I'm going to do?"

Again, the boy shook his head.

"Well, when I catch up with them . . . and sooner or later I will catch up with them . . . I'm going to kill them *both*."

The boy blinked and his eyes filled with tears. Then he turned his gaze toward the door and the rectangle of clear blue sky.

*　*　*

All that day Betty and her children watched the former
Holbrook lawman lie in their hogan. Sometimes he would
nod off in sleep, but only for a few seconds, and when
they would rise up to all run away, Slocum's head would
snap up and he'd curse them.

Finally, as darkness was falling, Betty stoked up the
cooking fire and gave the white man another big bowl of
mutton stew, only this time she added a few herbs that
she knew would make him very tired . . . even more tired
than he was now. And then he would fall into a deep and
dreamless sleep. The herbs belonged to Ira for medicine,
and she knew little about them except that they were
powerful.

"Stew tastes a little different than it did earlier," Slocum commented. "Whatever you added, it tastes even
better. Give me another bowl."

"All that is left in the pot is what I have for my children," Betty told him.

"Fill my damned bowl and the hell with your brats!"

Betty gave him the last of the stew. She watched him
devour it all as her children sat hungry and afraid. She
smiled at them often and hugged them close as darkness
fell.

"Damned good stew," Brady Slocum said, yawning
repeatedly. "Don't suppose you have any whiskey in this
hellhole?"

Betty shook her head.

"Not even any coffee?"

"No. Nothing to drink but water."

"It ain't water that I need, woman!"

She said nothing, and soon his chin was dropping onto

his chest. Once, he muttered, "Kill 'em both, by gawd," and then he yawned one last time and fell asleep.

Betty stood up and motioned for her children to all go outside. When they looked at her with questioning eyes, she made a quick motion with one finger across her throat so that they understood that their mother was going to do next. They hurried outside, and when the flap was closed and only Betty and Slocum were inside, she found the knife that Ira used to bleed out sheep before they were butchered.

A lamb is innocent; this man is evil.

And then with one quick, hard and sure motion, Betty cut the former marshal of Holbrook's throat from ear to ear.

Chapter 11

Longarm gazed in admiration at the incredible sandstone spires, arches and pinnacles that thrust hundreds of feet into the sky. One looked like the bow of a sailing ship, another like a huge bear surging up from Mother Earth. This was Monument Valley, so named because of its amazing red rock formations which towered high up against a cloudless sky. The land itself was harsh, arid and mostly rolling, crisscrossed with many dry arroyos and broken cliff faces. The bunch grasses in Monument Valley were short and tough; the sagebrush hunkered low to the ground because of the hard winds that regularly blew across this starkly beautiful country.

"I haven't seen a hogan or sign of anyone out here for days," Longarm told his friend.

"Too dry for raising cattle and horses. Sheep and goats can make it if the rains come."

"Why would Fergus Horn want to establish a trading post way up in this country if there are so few people?"

"More people farther up north along big San Juan and other rivers," Ira explained. "The whites who come down to this country want to stay hidden. Many people cross these valleys and make trade."

"In wool and hides?" Longarm asked.

"Yes, but also in guns and slaves captured from Mexico and other tribes. Many stolen horses are brought to this country."

"What about the rumor that Horn has found gold?"

Ira shrugged. "May be true. I've never found gold or silver."

"You ever prospect for any?"

Ira shook his head, and his face had a look of open contempt when he said, "Men are not meant to dig in ground like prairie dog or badger. Earth is not here for The People to dig holes in looking for white man's treasure."

"But you know what gold or silver is worth and what it can buy."

"I know. I see men kill other men for gold and silver."

"Do you know exactly where we can find Fergus Horn's trading post?"

Ira pointed to the northeast. "Two more days' ride. But it is a bad place."

"You can always turn around once it's in sight," Longarm told the half-breed. "You have a big family and they need your help and protection."

"Maybe I go back then, maybe I stay," Ira told him. "Two more days' ride and I will decide."

Two days later they had ridden through Monument Valley and they came upon a wide and deep canyon through which a meandering stream flowed. There was grass on the riverbanks and they saw many horses, sheep and cattle grazing up and down the broad and winding canyon.

"Over there," Ira said, pointing to a low rock structure sitting on a hump of red earth overlooking the north side of the red canyon. "That is Horn's trading post."

Longarm dismounted and tightened his cinch. He was a little sore from the long miles of riding but his wounds were healing and he felt strong. As he worked at tightening the cinch he studied the trading post, which was about a mile to the east.

"There are a lot of horses grazing along the riverbed. I see a herder or sentry up on the cliff and I wonder if that means that there are a lot of men staying at the trading post."

"Horn has maybe five or ten men who ride with him when he goes to steal horses and women. Once, I saw them from a long ways off and stayed out of their sight."

"Where were they headed?"

"To the San Juan River and up into Colorado. Maybe for more horses or women. Maybe to hunt for gold and silver."

Longarm finished tightening his cinch and then he dropped his stirrup and mounted his horse. "Fergus Horn will probably recognize me the minute we meet," he told his companion. "And when that happens he'll immediately want to know what I'm doing at his trading post and if I'm still working as a United States marshal. If I tell him the truth, he'll either try to kill me . . . or order me to leave at once."

"Maybe he is not there now," Ira said.

"Ira, can you go there and find out?"

The half-breed gave the matter some serious thought. "I will ride down into the canyon and come upon the herder. If he is Navajo, we will talk and he will tell me if Horn is here or not."

"That sounds like a good idea, but I'm worried about the sentry up on that cliff."

"You get closer to him and watch. If he raises his rifle to shoot me, shoot him first."

Before Longarm could form a reply, Ira was kicking his pinto pony down a steep dirt path toward the canyon's floor. Longarm watched him until he reached the bottom and then he put his own horse into a trot so that he could position himself up and behind the sentry.

Longarm dismounted behind some huge boulders and tied his horse to a piece of brush. He yanked his Winchester out of the saddle boot and hurried forward to where he could have a fair shot at the sentry, who was now standing up and watching Ira approach the herder.

Ira and the herder came together and Longarm could see that the herder was an Indian. The pair talked for quite some time while the sentry paced back and forth with agitation. Finally, Ira reined his pony around and waved at the sentry, then rode toward the trading post.

Because of the distance, Longarm could not hear what was said between Ira and the sentry, but after a few minutes the half-breed rode past the man and then on up to the rock-sided trading post. Ira dismounted and went inside, leaving Longarm to wonder what was going on.

Fifteen minutes later, Ira stepped out of the trading post and looked toward Longarm before making a gesture to indicate he should come on ahead.

"I wonder if that means that Fergus Horn is gone?" Longarm mused aloud. "Guess there's only one way I'm gonna find out."

He remounted his horse and rode around from behind the boulders. The sentry saw him and waved. Longarm waved back and trotted over to the trading post. He tied his horse beside the pinto at a long hitching rail and stepped up to Ira to whisper, "Is Horn here now?"

"No. He is gone with most of his men, but the herder does not know where he went or when he is to return."

"How many men are inside right now?"

"Four women and four men," Ira said. "The men are wearing guns and drinking whiskey. They said bad things to me when I went inside, but I closed my thoughts to them. I have been called those names many times."

"Ira, you should get on that pinto pony and head back to your family now," Longarm told the man. "I have a strong feeling that men are going to die here very soon."

"Maybe you."

"Maybe me," Longarm admitted. "But against four drunken gunmen, I like my chances."

"I will stand by this door and listen. If you need help, I will come inside with my rifle and help you kill those gunmen."

"If the shooting starts, just make sure that you don't kill me by mistake."

For some strange reason, Ira thought that was funny and he laughed right out loud.

Longarm checked his six-gun and thought momentarily about taking the big, double-barreled shotgun inside, but he rejected the idea. His thinking was that he hoped to pass himself off as just another loner traveling through hard country looking for a drink, maybe a game of cards and a bit of friendly conversation.

Exiting from bright sunlight and going into a dimly lit interior room filled with gunmen was always a dicey proposition, and Longarm took a deep breath to compose himself before he stepped inside.

His appearance caused conversation to die and Longarm said, "Good afternoon, gents. Any whiskey in this place to be bought?"

"Yeah, there's plenty of damned whiskey. But we're real particular who drinks among us."

"That speaks highly of your character," Longarm said, eyes straining in the dim light. "I've come a long way and I'm plenty hungry and thirsty."

"That half-breed that slunk in and out of here riding along with you?" one of the men drinking at the rough-cut bar asked.

"As a matter of fact, I only met him a few miles back and he just sort of tagged along with me."

"You in the habit of keeping company with his kind?" another gun man demanded, setting his drink on the bar top and glaring hard at Longarm.

"I found his company acceptable. He doesn't talk much but he's part Navajo and I figured he might be useful."

"He ain't welcome in here."

Longarm forced a smile. "Ira isn't in here now. How about a drink of whiskey to wash the dust out of my throat? I'll even buy you boys a round or two."

The gunmen liked that idea well enough to relax. "Rosa! Get this stranger a bottle and pour us another round."

A chair back in the corner scraped against the sandstone floor and a heavyset woman missing most of her teeth, who might have been Indian or perhaps Mexican, appeared. "Are you also hungry, senor?"

"Whiskey will be fine for the time being," Longarm replied, aware that the men at the bar were taking his full measure.

His eyesight was improving rapidly and Longarm could see now well enough to navigate himself around a pickle barrel and up to the empty section of the bar. He leaned his right hip against it so that the gun on his left hip facing butt forward was in plain sight. The woman found a glass and a bottle and plunked them both on the bar top.

"One dollar for you and these men, senor," she said, gesturing to the others. "And when you finish, maybe you and that Indian had better go away."

"Rosa, shut your mouth," one of the men growled. "If the man has money, he can stay just as long as he keeps buying us all drinks."

Longarm poured his glass and then went down to the four men and offered the bottle. There was no thank-you or even a nod of appreciation.

"Where you from?" one of the men asked.

"Holbrook."

"That a fact?"

"It is," Longarm assured the man.

"What is your business up here?"

Longarm tossed down his whiskey and then turned to stare at the man. "Where I come from, men aren't in the habit of asking other men either their business or where they came from or are headed."

The man flushed with anger and he stepped away from the bar with his hand poised over the butt of his six-gun.

"Mister, I don't give a good gawdamn what men do where you come from. I just asked you a question and I expect a quick and civil answer!"

This sure wasn't the first time in his lawman's career that someone had demanded to know his business, and so Longarm had a quick and ready answer. "I'm a speculator," he said.

"A *what?*"

"A speculator. I speculate in anything that I can buy cheap and then turn it around and sell high for a sizable profit. That includes Indian jewelry, rugs, horses, watches, knives, gold, silver, guns . . . whatever. If the price is right, I'll buy it for resale."

The man who had confronted Longarm frowned. "You're nothin' but a trader is what you are. Speculator sounds way too grand a handle for a fella that just buys up things to make a quick profit."

"Call me a trader if you want," Longarm said nonchalantly. "It doesn't matter a whit to me. Do any of you gentlemen have anything you'd like to sell me cheap?"

The one who seemed to be the leader of this collection of ugly misfits stood about six foot tall with broad, sloping shoulders and a bull neck. Like his companions he was so unwashed that he stunk, and his shirt was stained with dirt, grease and all kinds of unpleasant things. He had a beard, but it was scraggly and matted and his hair was black, stringy and long.

"What do they call you?" Longarm asked.

"Bull." He hammered his thick chest. "That's what I'm called. What's your handle, stranger?"

"Custis." Longarm turned to the other three, who were eyeballing him with suspicion. "And your fine friends?"

Bull thought about it for a moment and then relaxed. "The little fella is Shorty, the fat one is Gordo and the other is Dennison."

Longarm knew better than to offer his hand in friendship. And when he had sized them all up, he figured that the tall, lean one with the angular face was probably the most dangerous. Yes, Dennison looked like a professional gunslinger with his rig tied to his right hip and that fancy holster.

"Well, boys," Longarm said, mustering up all the cheeriness he could in his voice. "Let's have another round of drinks on me!"

The four men exchanged glances and Bull said, "The first bottle ain't gonna last very long."

"I'll buy more," Longarm told him. "I'll buy as many as we need to get stinking drunk."

Bull actually smiled, though when he did he displayed two missing front teeth and a whole lot of rotting in his mouth. "Maybe you're gonna be all right, Custis."

"Glad to hear that, but I'm just passing through. I had been told that there was a fella named Fergus Horn who owned this trading post, and that his wife was quite the looker. I believe her name is Veronica."

Bull's smile faded. "Mr. Horn doesn't like men looking at his wife . . . or even speaking to her. Best that you know that right now so you don't get your throat cut or your balls sliced off."

"Oh," Longarm said, throwing up both hands in a gesture of complete agreement. "I would never try to insult or get familiar with another man's wife . . ." He winked. "Unless she's pretty and willing."

Dennison barked a laugh and so did Shorty and Gordo.

Bull wasn't sure how to react, so he just picked up the bottle and poured himself another drink until his glass overflowed. Then, turning to Longarm and raising his glass, he said, "Here's to life and to women, the prettier the better. And when are Mr. Horn and his wife coming back? I'd like to see if I can do a little trading with the man."

"Mr. Horn doesn't tell us when he leaves or where he's goin' or when he's comin' back. All we do is to make sure that when he's gone nobody comes here and robs his trading post." Bull made a gesture to include the big room. "As you can plainly see, there is hundreds of dollars' worth of goods here. Sugar, beans, flour by the barrel but also crackers and blankets, rifles, picks, shovels, bullets and knives. There's just about everything a man could ask for or need in this country."

Longarm nodded in agreement.

Bull said, "What did you buy and sell in Holbrook, Custis?"

"Huh?"

"You said you had ridden up from Holbrook. That's maybe three hundred miles across some hard, damned dry country. Are you tellin' me that you did that all by your lonesome?"

"Yeah," Longarm said, stiffening as if he had been grievously insulted and moving his hand closer to his six-gun. "And are you telling me that you think I'm a *liar*?"

Bull's smile died and he shot a glance at Dennison, who stepped away from the bar. "I'm not calling you anything. Why, I'd be seven times a damned fool to insult the man who is buyin' the drinks, wouldn't I?"

"You would," Longarm told him. "And you don't look like a fool to me, and neither do your three friends."

"Then let's all just calm down and get drunk," Bull said. "It's always a pleasure to meet a new friend."

"I agree," Longarm said, relieved that Dennison had turned back to his drink. "But you boys still haven't told me if you have anything that you want to sell."

"I've got a pocket watch I'd probably be willin' to part with for the right price," Gordo offered, dragging a dull brass watch of little value out of his grimy vest. "I'd probably take only five dollars for 'er."

"Yeah," Longarm said, barely giving the cheap watch a glance. "I'll just bet that you would. But I'm not interested in pocket watches. I was hoping that I might find some quality Navajo gold or silver jewelry."

Shorty scoffed. "Hell, we don't wear jewelry, but the Indians have a real hankerin' for turquoise and silver jewelry. You can buy a barrelful of that shiny crap for only a few dollars."

"Maybe I will," Longarm said, signaling Rosa to bring them another bottle. "Let's drink up, and then I'm going to see if I can get one of those women to rustle me up some food."

Dennison snickered. "For pocket change, any one of 'em will rustle up your bean and pump it dry, if you want. They ain't all that bad with their tongues and mouths, either. They ain't got hardly no teeth to nip you with, so you don't have to worry about a bite."

The four men chuckled, and Longarm turned to see all the woman stiffen at the crude insults. "Well," he said, "I'm not interested in that as much as I am in getting drunk and fed."

"Rosa!" Bull shouted. "Get this man a plate of beans and beef to go with his whiskey!"

Rosa headed out of the room into what Longarm supposed was a kitchen. He followed her a few steps and called out, "And when you fetch me up a plate, take another to that half-breed fella outside. His name is Ira."

"Why, Custis, a few minutes ago you said he wasn't any damned friend of yours," Gordo challenged.

"He isn't. But Ira did help guide me across the reservation, and I kind of feel obligated to make sure that he at least eats."

"He ain't nothin' but a dirty redskin."

Longarm wanted badly to tell Gordo that he and his friends were actually the real filthy and dirty ones, but he kept his silence a moment, then turned to look at Rosa. "Feed Ira and tell him I'll be around tomorrow."

She nodded and Longarm almost thought he saw the hint of a smile cross her round, sad face.

Chapter 12

It was well after midnight and Longarm was feeling no pain when he exited the trading post with the four gunmen passed out on the dirt floor. He took a few deep breaths, then headed out toward the corrals, wanting to speak to Ira.

Gripping the rough poles of the corral, he turned back to look at the trading post and realized he was seeing double. In his determination to get the four gunmen dead drunk, he'd gotten pretty drunk himself.

"Ira?"

The half-breed appeared like ghost out of the night. "I'm here."

"As we expected, Fergus Horn and his wife are gone. I couldn't find out where they went or when they'll return because I'm sure that neither Bull nor any of the others knows the answer to that question. What I *did* learn is that Mrs. Horn is still alive and she is with Horn. I kind of got the impression that she had tried to run away a few times, so now Horn takes her with him whenever he leaves."

"Makes sense, I guess."

"I don't know if they're looking for gold or silver . . . or maybe just trading," Longarm continued. "But what I do know is that they admitted that Horn was intent on stirring up a hornet's nest on your reservation."

Ira simply nodded.

Longarm added, "We can wait here for them to return or we can try and find them. I understand that you are an excellent tracker."

"I can track men, horses . . . most anything."

"Then I think we ought to leave this trading post and see if you can pick up the tracks that Horn and his wife left. I'm sure that you can tell us how many men are riding with Horn and perhaps we can find out exactly what they are up to."

"Are you going to kill those four hired gunmen inside?"

Longarm shook his head. "I'm a United States Marshal and I can't kill anyone unless they try to kill me first."

"They will try . . . sooner or later."

"I expect so."

"Then you should kill them now. I will help."

"No," Longarm said flatly. "They're dead drunk, and killing them would be equal to an execution. I can't have that on my conscience and I won't put it on yours, either."

Ira shrugged to let him know that his conscience could stand the load.

"Let's go into the trading post and help ourselves to what we need. The women won't object."

"No," Ira said. "They won't object. They are captives, and if we leave them here they might kill those four men before daybreak and then run off."

"Would they get far?"

"Depends on how soon Horn returns and finds them missing. If they have three or four days, the slave women might get away and not be caught."

Longarm considered what the half-breed had just told him. "Do you think that they would actually kill those four?"

Ira nodded. "Yes, and they would kill those men tonight. They have suffered much from those men."

"I could talk to them. Try to make them promise to leave the four men alone and unhurt."

"They wouldn't promise you anything," Ira told him. "They *will* kill those four. They already told me that they have wanted to do that for a long time. But mostly they would like to kill Horn."

"If the slave women are so determined to exact blood revenge on Bull, Dennison, Gordo and Shorty, then we'll just have to take them with us. If the women commit cold-blooded murder, even I couldn't stop them from eventually being caught and hanged."

"It would not be good to take the women with us," Ira told him.

"What other choice do we have?"

Ira did not reply, but the idea of taking four slave women to try and track down Fergus Horn and however many gunmen he had riding with him was very troubling.

After further discussion, Longarm and Ira decided that they would take all the trading post horses so that when the four gunmen woke up they would have no way to leave or create additional problems.

"I have spoken to the slave women and they are happy to ride with us tonight to go after Horn. The handsome one named Josie says she is a good shot and she asks if she could have the honor of killing Horn. They say that they will hitch up four ponies to a buckboard, and we have two extra to tie to the wagon. We'll take plenty of food and ammunition, and all the guns they find in the trading post."

"Good," Longarm said. "But I can't have Josie or any of them just opening fire on Horn and his men. That simply won't do."

"When we find Horn and his gunmen, either they will kill us . . . or we will kill them first."

Longarm's head was pounding and he listened to a coyote's mournful cry, which, at the moment, reflected his own dark and melancholy mood. "Ira, I'm hoping to confront Fergus Horn and get to the bottom of what he is doing up here. Also, there is some real concern that his ex-wife, Veronica, is being held against her free will. She wrote a desperate note and it managed to reach Denver. That's why I was sent here . . . to find that woman and make sure that she is all right and not being held a captive. I'm also here to stop any trouble that Horn might be causing among the Navajo."

"We will find these men," Ira promised. "But I do not like the idea of the slave women coming with us."

"I don't like it either, but what choice do I have if they are so determined to murder Gordo, Dennison, Bull and Shorty?"

"Let them kill those four."

"I already told you that I can't do that. So let's quit the talk and get ready to travel."

The half-breed went into the trading post to speak with the women again and tell them of the plan. Longarm walked out to the rim of the canyon and sat down on a rock. Things were moving damned fast, and this idea of the four slave women coming along with him really was an unexpected complication he did not need. Josie was the pretty one, but the moment he had laid eyes upon her he knew she was filled with hatred for the trading post whites and would kill them at the first opportunity.

"What a mess," he said to himself as he massaged his throbbing temples. "I can't believe what I'm getting myself into."

Longarm enjoyed a cigar now and then, and he had bought a couple in the trading post a short while ago while drinking with the four gunmen. Now, he lit one of the cigars and immediately grimaced because the tobacco was so foul. He tossed the cigar out into space, got up and trudged back toward the trading post. Out in front was a horse watering trough, and he dunked his head into it just to clear his brain.

"It's gonna be interesting the next few days," he said to the moon. "And I got a bad feeling that I've bitten off a whole lot more than I can chew."

Ira came outside. "The slave women have tied up the four men hand and foot. They will not be able to get free for many hours after they awake. It will give us even more time."

"I don't imagine they'll be in any shape to *walk* after us."

"No walking for those men. After tying them, the slave women took off their boots and cut the bottoms of their feet." Ira smiled. "They will not walk anywhere for a long time."

Longarm's jaw dropped. "The slave women cut the soles of their bare feet?

Ira dipped his chin. "They wanted to cut their throats, but cutting their feet is also good."

"I didn't even hear those four men scream."

"Men gagged. Hit over the heads, too."

Longarm shook his head. "We'd better pack up the buckboard and get moving before the slave women do something *really* terrible."

"Like cutting off their balls?" Ira asked with a slight smile.

"Yeah, exactly."

"They wanted to do that, too," Ira confessed. "But I thought they might all bleed to death, and I understand that the white man's court would call it murder and you said they would hang for that."

"I sure did!" Longarm shook the cold water from his hair and growled. "I want to be out of here before daybreak, so let's get that buckboard hitched up and loaded. I have a feeling this is going to be a long, hard day."

"Slave women very happy to leave this trading post. Horn make them work very hard in the day and then keep all his men happy after dark. Slave women say that, after we kill Horn and his men, we all can finally go home."

"Yeah," Longarm agreed, thinking of Molly Malloy and his comfortable Denver apartment. "It will be good if we all can go home."

Chapter 13

Because he'd gotten a tad tight the night before while trying to extract any information he could about Fergus Horn and his troublemaking, Longarm was feeling rather punk that morning when they finally left the trading post. He'd sent Ira off to the northeast to begin looking for Horn's tracks, but Longarm wasn't too hopeful there would be any to find, given the heavy rainstorms that had recently ravaged this vast red-rock country.

The four former slave women were silent all morning as Rosa drove the ill-matched team of Indian ponies along. The ponies, it turned out, had never really been put in harness before, and they'd put up one hell of a fight when they were asked to pull the buckboard and four women. But Josie had proven to be excellent with horses, and after a half hour or so, she'd managed to get them all harnessed and pulling more or less in tandem.

Every time Longarm peered over his shoulder at the runty Indian ponies, the creaky buckboard and the four former slave women, he had to shake his head in amazement and dismay. This was *not* how a highly regarded federal marshal was supposed to conduct a manhunt. After all the years that Longarm had worn a badge, he could not remember being in such a pathetic fix, nor had he heard of any other marshal getting into such a predicament. Yet, what else could he do but take these women along? Ira had told him without hesitation that the slave women would have murdered the four gunmen back at that damned trading post.

All day long they rode, following the fresh tracks and occasional signs left by Ira as he ranged miles ahead looking for Horn and his company of men and perhaps the beautiful Veronica. The weather stayed fair and they did not see another living soul, only an occasional rattlesnake, hawk or coyote.

Longarm's mind often drifted back to Denver and Molly Malloy. He wondered if she was spending a lot of her free time living in his apartment, which was nicer and a bit more accommodating than her own. And he wondered if she still wanted to marry him. But mostly, Longarm wondered what she would think and say if she could see him right now out in this empty country with only the companionship of four hard women out for a bloody revenge.

"She'd probably think I was completely insane to have allowed myself to get into such a bad fix," Longarm said to his horse as he rode just ahead of the trading post buckboard. "And she'd be right."

Toward evening the land began to change. The sagebrush gave way to some low grasses, and they saw a few antelope off in the distance. Ira was still miles ahead of them following tracks that Longarm couldn't see, steady toward Colorado.

"It's time to stop!" he called just before the sun was setting. "Let's make up a camp and see if Ira comes in for the night."

Rosa hauled on the lines and the mismatched Indian ponies came to a grateful and ungainly stop. The place that Longarm had chosen to camp was protected from the wind behind some high rocks and a low hill. It was also near a spring that fed an acre of good grass for the ponies. Longarm had been out on enough manhunts to know that you didn't build a campfire where it could be seen from a great distance.

The women spoke decent English, and they were more than experienced and capable camp cooks and tenders. Josie had even been thoughtful enough to bring a nice bedroll for Longarm to sleep upon; the women had not been bashful about taking everything they would need from Horn's trading post. So that night as the stars came out and the campfire blazed under a canopy of stars, the meal and the talk between the women was almost cheerful.

Longarm's hangover had left him by mid-afternoon, but when the women pulled out a bottle of whiskey and another of tequila, he declined to drink. "Think I'll just pass on that tonight, thank you very much."

The women laughed and passed the tequila around and around between themselves. In the light of the campfire, Longarm could see that they almost seemed to have grown younger since they left the hated trading post that same morning. Rosa appeared almost girlish, even though she was past her prime. Juanita was quiet and a little bit older, but she seemed to be in excellent spirits and wasn't in the least bashful about drinking more than her share of tequila. Teresa was the oldest of the four and wanted to talk about her childhood in a small Mexican village where her father was a farmer and her mother weaved to make extra money for the children.

Josie was the only one who had bathed in the spring and washed her hair. She'd allowed one of the women to comb it dry and now it glistened like a raven's wing. She was, Longarm thought, quite a beauty now that she had washed her hair and body and considered herself free. Her laughter was light and musical, and the other women clearly deferred to her when she offered something to say. Longarm learned that Josie had been born and raised on a small ranch down near Tucson. The Apache had raided her ranch five years earlier and killed all of her family. Terrified and alone, she had been taken down into Mexico and sold to be the mistress of a rich old lecher with three equally lecherous sons. Josie had finally escaped Mexico and by night had walked north across the border, only to be caught and eventually sold to Fergus Horn. It was clear that she had been his favorite mistress, and Longarm wondered what Veronica Horn had done and felt about that.

"I'm getting sleepy," he announced after an excellent dinner of fried corn, beef and beans. "I'm going to turn in, and I'd advise you women not to stay up drinking the rest of that tequila and whiskey tonight."

"Why shouldn't we?" Josie had challenged. "For too long we have had to watch man-pigs drink until they were too drunk to do anything but vomit and fart."

"I'm sure that is true," Longarm said, "but Fergus Horn didn't drink himself into a stupor every night, did he?"

"No," Rosa reluctantly confessed. "That one and Dennison, they always drank only a few glasses. That way they could hump us all they wanted when the others had passed out drunk."

"How many men do you think Horn has riding with him?" Longarm asked. "Surely you saw him leave the trading post."

"He left with two gunmen. But I think he was going to meet more in Colorado," Rosa said.

"And what about his former wife, the beautiful Veronica?"

"She is probably dead by now," Josie said looking grim. "She was a real lady but she never looked down upon us captives as if we were trash. She kept trying to escape the trading post. But everyone knew that if they helped her they would be tortured to death."

"Was she in good health and of a sound mind the last time that you saw her leave with Horn?"

All four women shook their heads. "The lady was very thin and weak. She would not eat much and we had to beg her to stay alive. I think that she wanted to die."

Longarm nodded with understanding. "Did she ever tell you that she was the daughter of the former governor of Colorado?"

"No," the women all said at once. Then Josie said, "But I could tell that she had lived a good life and had a fine education. She spoke better than anyone at the trading post, and whenever she could manage it, her face was in a book. Horn would grow angry because she wanted to be left alone to read . . . and often cry. He would slap her in the face and sometimes lock her in a storage room for days."

"Did she ever try to kill him?" Longarm asked.

"Once she tried to poison him, but the rat poison was very old and Horn just got very sick. He never knew that the lady had poisoned him, and if he had known I think he would have killed her. As it was, she seemed always to be near death."

"That is right," Juanita agreed. "The lady was so thin you could see the blue veins in her hands, arms and face. Her hair, which had once been long and shiny—like Josie's hair only of a light color— grew dull and began to fall out. Horn would demand that we brush her hair every night and feed her so that she did not look like a skeleton. We tried to do this, but it was impossible."

"Yes, very difficult," Teresa added. "We were in a bad place with bad men and our lives were very . . . very sad. But always, we knew that the lady from Colorado even had it worse than ourselves."

"When Horn got mad at the lady and she wouldn't do what he ordered, he would threaten to give her to Gordo or Bull for the night. This made the lady cry and shake with fear just as if she had seen a ghost."

Longarm listened and his anger rose like a bile in his throat. "If I can save Miss Sutton, I will make it my highest priority."

"Your what?" Josie asked, frowning.

"My number one thing of importance will be to save the woman and return her to Colorado, if that is what she chooses."

"You can do that if you want," Juanita said. "But the most important thing for *us* is to kill Horn and his men."

"How many of you have ever even fired a weapon?" Longarm asked with plenty of skepticism.

All four of them raised their hands.

"How many of you have shot a gun or a rifle at a man with the intention of killing him?" Longarm asked.

Juanita and Josie raised their hands in the firelight, and Rosa said, "I stabbed a man to death in the New Mexico Territory. He was a very bad man and he was hurting me so I stabbed him in the guts. He died screaming and begging for his mother. I ran away and was never caught for that, and I never was sorry that he died in such pain."

Longarm studied Rosa's round and troubled face. "How old are you?"

"Twenty-seven. But I have lived much longer than that, if you understand what I am telling you."

"I understand. What about you, Juanita?"

She looked away for a moment in embarrassment. "I am almost thirty. I have sisters and brothers in Mexico, and if I live through this I will go back to live with them and ask forgiveness from the mission priest."

"You were taken against your will and therefore in my opinion you have no need for shame or forgiveness."

"I have sinned very bad and done everything a woman can do with a man . . . and worse."

"Not because you liked it, though," Longarm argued.

"I liked it sometimes," Josie said, eyes flashing at Longarm in proud and open defiance. "I hated Horn and what he did to me, but I have loved many men well and am not ashamed."

"Good. Where will you go if we live through the fight we are almost sure to have?"

"I will go all the way to California," Josie announced with a smile. "I have an uncle there who has a rancho near the ocean. He always liked me."

"He probably liked you too much," Juanita said to the accompanying laughter of the others.

Josie shook her head with exasperation. "You women think there is only one thing that men want from women like us."

"We don't just think it," Teresa countered, "we *know* what they always want, and it is the little treasure box we have between our legs!"

"The *stink* box," Juanita scoffed.

"Stink or not, it is what we have that they most want from us."

Longarm was feeling a bit embarrassed by this bawdy female conversation. "I think I'll go to sleep. Ira may come in later tonight, but I wouldn't be surprised if he is camped out there ahead of us a few miles. We might not see him for days."

"Does that handsome half-breed already have a wife?" Josie asked, causing the other women to laugh again at her.

"He does. A good wife and a big family."

"I thought so," Josie said not bothering to hide her disappointment. "He does not say much but you can tell he is a good and brave man."

"Yes," Longarm said. "He is. We're lucky to have Ira scouting for us. For all that we know, Horn and his men could be just a few miles up ahead and on their way back to the trading post. We could stumble upon them and all be killed or captured."

"I would rather die than be captured again!" Josie spat.

"Me too," Rosa said. "I would kill myself before I would let them take me back to that gawdamn trading post."

The other two women nodded their heads in agreement and looked at Longarm for support. He stared into the campfire for a moment and then he said, "I promise you that you will not be taken captive and made to be slaves again by Fergus Horn or anyone else. You each have suffered too much already and deserve some happiness."

"How can you make that promise if you are killed right away by one of them?" Teresa demanded. "You are not a god, and you bleed and can be killed by just one bullet."

"I know that," Longarm said. "I am anything but a god, and I make many mistakes. I have been shot, stabbed and beaten, but I have always managed to stay alive and defeat my enemies. I can do it this time with your help and the help of Ira. It would just help a lot if I knew what we are going to come up against."

"You mean," Rosa said, "how many fighters Horn has with him?"

"That's exactly what I mean," Longarm replied. "But none of you seem to have any idea of that, so we'll just have to wait and see. I can tell you that when we find Horn, the killing will be swift. Those men have used you, and they will not feel guilty or show any mercy because you are women. They will kill you as quickly as they would kill a scorpion or rattlesnake."

"We know that," Josie said. "We know we must be willing to fight to the death or have no chance at all."

"All right," Longarm said, coming to his feet and picking up his bedroll. "Just as long as we all understand each other. And if any of you wants to leave in the morning, we will cut a pony loose for you and you can just ride away from this bad trouble."

"We will stick together and kill those mean, fucking men," Josie vowed. "But you had better not get killed first."

"I won't," he said. "Goodnight."

The women all said goodnight and Longarm took his bedroll a short distance from the fire. As he lay down under the stars in darkness, he could hear their animated conversation. They were telling each other about how it would be best to wound Horn and his gunmen so that they could kill them slow and castrate them while they were helpless. That kind of talk bothered Longarm, because when the shooting started in earnest, these slave women needed to understand that you didn't aim to wound your hated enemy, you aimed for his heart to kill him with one bullet. In the morning, he would have to make sure these four women understood this clearly.

He drifted off to sleep listening to their boisterous conversation and laughter fueled by the liquor. Longarm was pretty certain that they had finished their bottle of tequila and had already started on the bottle of whiskey. And he probably should have gotten up and taken their bottle away but he just didn't have the heart. After all, these women had suffered terrible insults and indignities by the men they were now determined to kill. And this being their first night of freedom, they more than deserved to drink, laugh and celebrate.

Sometime in the night Josie crawled under his bedroll and unbuttoned his pants. By the time Longarm was fully awake, she was on him like a wildcat. And even though he should have pushed her away, she had his manhood in her hand and was shoving it up into her "little treasure" so adeptly that he simply didn't care to utter even a little protest.

"I knew you would be long and hard for me tonight," Josie panted in his ear as she began to pump up and down on his stiff rod. "I could see in your eyes that you love having a young and pretty Mexican woman whenever you get the chance."

"I wasn't expecting this tonight," he managed to say.

"I don't believe you, lawman. You wanted me the first time you laid your eyes on my face, my chest and my legs. I could tell you did, and it will do no good to argue."

Longarm pulled her close and began to hump upward into her wet and slick treasure. "You had me pegged right," he grunted.

"Are you married?" Josie asked, working her little butt faster.

"No."

"Maybe you would like to go with me to California and see my uncle's rancho and the ocean. We could make love every afternoon on a sandy beach."

"If we did it like this, you would drive sand far up my asshole," he reasoned.

Josie threw back her head and laughed. The other women would have heard her, but she clearly did not care.

After a few minutes of her working on him, Longarm rolled Josie onto her back and began to hammer at her with more enthusiasm and pleasure than he would have thought possible under these difficult circumstances. But then, when you had the chance to do it and you faced death in the days to come, you might as well cast caution to the wind and let the beast in you stand up straight and howl.

Longarm worked on Josie until he could not stand it another moment, and when his body convulsed and he implanted her with his torrents of seed, he threw his head back and howled at the moon.

"You are plenty much of a man," Josie said when she had finished satisfying herself. "And I am plenty much of a woman. Do you think I am pretty?"

"I do."

"But you still don't want to go with me to California after what we have just done together?"

"I can't."

"Why not? You said that you do not have a wife."

"I have a woman in Denver waiting for my return."

"Ha!" Josie crowed. "Let her wait! If you come with me to California and you are not happy, I can always find another big handsome man and you can return to your woman in Denver."

"I don't want to go to California. I have a job in Denver."

Josie rolled him off and smiled. "Maybe I will go

with you to Denver instead of California. Is your woman there prettier or better at fucking than I am?"

"Not really."

"Then you see! I will take you from her and we will see what we think of Denver together."

Longarm knew there was no point in arguing this matter with Josie. After all that she had been through at the trading post, she hungered for a good . . . even just a decent man.

And besides, the night was still young and he thought he might just want to get back inside her again a time or two before daybreak.

Chapter 14

Longarm and Josie were awakened just after dawn by Ira, who was stoking the campfire and making himself a breakfast of pancakes and pork fried in fat.

"Got any coffee made yet?" Longarm asked the half-breed as he stood up and stretched.

Ira looked at Josie. "I figured you'd pick Josie, and you sure didn't waste any time about it."

"Maybe she picked me," Longarm said, managing a sheepish grin as he pulled on his pants, boots and shirt. "Did you find Fergus Horn and his gunmen?"

"I did," Ira replied. "Or at least I found where they were two days ago."

By the tone of Ira's voice and the hard look on the man's darkly handsome face, Longarm immediately knew that there was bad news coming. "What did you find?"

"I found a family that had been massacred. Horn and his men made it out to look like it was an Indian raid, but it wasn't. The man of the family had a Navajo hatchet buried deep in the back of his head, his woman had been raped and murdered and there were two children that were shot out in a little cornfield. Their cabin had been burned to the ground and their livestock all shot full of arrows."

"Damn!" Longarm whispered, "Are you *sure* it was Fergus Horn and his bunch?"

"Oh, I'm sure all right. And there was little doubt that they were trying to make it look like an Indian raiding party. I buried the family and cleaned up things the best that I could. But anyone who doesn't know how to read signs would swear that Navajo were the raiders."

"So Horn really is trying to stir up trouble between the whites and the Navajo."

"There is no doubt about it," Ira said. "But when I left, I made sure that there were no false signs to be found. I even extracted the arrows from the livestock and burned them."

"Good," Longarm said. "I always knew that Fergus Horn was a hard man, but I never thought he'd go so wrong that he'd attack and murder women and children."

"He did it, all right."

"How many riders are with him?"

"As near as I can tell there are nine. One of them is probably the white woman you want to help."

"Veronica." Longarm shook his head. "I can't even imagine the state of her mind if she had to sit on her horse and helplessly watch the wife being raped and the entire family being murdered."

"It would have been very bad for anyone to watch," Ira said. "Bad to bury them, too." Ira waited a moment as if considering his next words. "Coyotes were there before me, and they were hungry."

"I get the picture," Longarm said bitterly. "Did you follow the trail they made after they murdered the homesteaders?"

"Still to the northeast and Colorado."

"I wonder what they are after next," Longarm mused aloud. "I'm sure they didn't ride that far just to murder a poor family and steal their pitiful belongings."

"Hell no, they didn't!" It was Josie and she was wiggling into her skirt, naked breasts toned gold in the morning sunrise. "I think they have a boom town in mind to hit next."

Both Longarm and Ira turned to her. "What makes you think that?" Longarm asked.

"I heard a name and some drunken talk the night before they left. Horn was on me when a man came into the room to watch us, and now I remember Horn saying something like, 'Get out of here and get ready for Elk Creek.'"

"It's a Colorado mining town," Ira said. "I've never been there, but I talked to a Ute friend of mine passing through Holbrook, and he told me that there was a big gold strike at Elk Creek."

"I wonder if Horn intends to buy some mining claims there or . . . or simply attack and rob a prosperous mining town?" Longarm asked aloud. "With Fergus Horn leading eight experienced gunmen, and given his element of surprise, he could probably pull it off. Then again, he might just plan to rob a gold mine."

"Only one way to answer the question," Ira said. "But they got a pretty big lead on us."

"All right," Longarm said, "let's do our best to cut the lead."

"Isn't going to happen pulling that old buckboard," Josie told them. "But if we repacked everything we might manage to make it."

"How would we do that?" Longarm asked.

Josie replied. "We have six ponies altogether. We women can ride four of them bareback and we'll make blanket slings to strap rifles, ammunition and provisions on the other two ponies. You and Ira have good saddle horses, and there's no reason we can't move a whole lot faster than we've been moving."

"I agree," Longarm said. "That buckboard has really been slowing us down and it looks ready to fall apart. Wake up your friends, Josie."

"They're not going to be all that easy to wake," she said, placing her fingers to both sides of her head. "We celebrated maybe a little too much last night."

"I know how you feel," Longarm answered. "But celebration time is over, and what we'll be facing next is going to require clear thinking. I'm sure you just heard what Ira said he found up ahead."

"I heard," Josie answered. "And I'll be sure to tell the other women about it, which will make them all the more determined to kill Horn."

"Did you also hear that he has nine riders?"

"Yes, but one of them is the lady, so that means that each of us only has to kill one or two."

Longarm almost smiled. "I like your attitude, Josie."

She shook her lovely, bare breasts enticingly. "That isn't all that you like about me, Marshal."

"No," he confessed, "it sure isn't."

Josie turned to Ira, who looked extremely uncomfortable. "Are you *sure* that you have a wife and a bunch of children?"

"I'm sure," Ira said, turning away from the campfire and forgetting all about having breakfast.

Except for Juanita, the former slave women were good riders. Longarm tried to force the pace again and again, but each time the ponies began to trot, rifles, guns and other provisions would bounce out of the slings. So they had to pretty much keep to a steady walk, and that day Longarm guessed they might have traveled about twenty miles.

"I wish we could move along quicker," he told Ira that night around their campfire. "We're traveling faster than we could have with the buckboard, but not nearly as fast as I'd hoped."

"You and I could ride on ahead," Ira suggested. "The women could follow behind."

"That's not a bad idea," Longarm replied. "I sure am eager to get to Elk Creek, because I have a real strong feeling that something bad is going to happen when Fergus and his men arrive ahead of us."

"Then let's go on ahead," Ira said. "The women are complaining about all the sores that they're getting from riding bareback. They're greasing themselves up tonight and they're not in very good spirits."

"They're probably still a little hung over from the drinking they did last night."

"How about you?" Ira asked. "Your eyes look like two burnt-out holes in a blanket. You didn't get much sleep last night."

"I'll do better tonight," he vowed.

"Don't count on it," Ira said. "That Josie woman is man-hungry."

Longarm nodded. "Ordinarily, I'd think that was wonderful. But I'm completely whipped tonight and I need to get more sleep."

"Then you'd better take your bedroll out into the brush and hide," Ira advised. "That's what I'm going to do."

"Maybe we should just saddle up our horses again and ride a few miles up ahead to sleep."

"Good idea."

And that was what they did despite the howls of protest from the four women. And in the morning, before the slave women could repack and catch up with them, Longarm and Ira were back in the saddle and galloping toward Elk Creek.

At noon they topped a rocky pine-covered ridge to look out toward the bustling Colorado mining town.

"Looks like an ant colony that has been stirred up," Ira observed. "Sure are a lot of white people."

"I wonder if Fergus and his men have already done their damage," Longarm mused aloud.

"Only one way to find out."

"You're right." Longarm glanced back over his shoulder. He did not expect to see the four angry women whom he had abandoned the night before and he did not see them. But he knew without the slightest doubt that they were coming as fast as their sore and blistered butts could handle the pace. And Longarm also knew that, when they caught up with him in Elk Creek or further on down the road, they would be almost as ready to shoot him as they were Fergus Horn and his murdering gun hands.

Chapter 15

Longarm and Ira rode down from the pine-studded hills into Elk Creek, and it was immediately evident that the town was in a great turmoil. Four caskets draped with American flags were sitting under one of the only porches on the main street, and there wasn't a smile or greeting to be found among the inhabitants. Some whores working out of the Red Dog Saloon were sitting on the sidewalk and two of them were crying.

"Hey!" Longarm called to an old, white-bearded fellow watching over the caskets with his head bowed as if in prayer. "What happened here?"

The old man's head snapped up and his eyes were red and swollen as he glared at the two newcomers. "Ain't you heard?"

"We just rode in from the Arizona Territory. But it looks like you folks have had some terrible trouble just recently."

"You could call it trouble, I call it a gawdamn shit-storm!" the old man snapped. "You see these four caskets, don't ya?"

"Yes."

"Well, they were four of our best men who were gunned down in that cabin over yonder that used to be the town's only bank. One was the banker himself, Mr. Ollie Peterson; another was a bank guard and the last two fellas were just unlucky enough to be inside the bank when the holdup gang burst through the door with guns blazing."

Longarm glanced sideways at Ira, then back at the old man who spat a thick stream of tobacco at his feet, then wiped his eyes with the back of his dirty sleeve. "Those murdering sonsabitches didn't even give anyone inside the bank the chance to throw up their hands and surrender. No sir! Them dirty bastards just shot 'em down like rabid dogs."

"Did they wear masks?"

"Oh, hell yeah! They were *all* masked. But before they could all mount up and ride off untouched, Mike O'Leary did manage to shoot one off his horse. Shot the sonofabitch right through the heart! But the others all rode away and left Elk Creek busted."

"Did anyone in Elk Creek form a posse and ride after them?" Longarm asked.

"Sure! And that's when the story gets even more awful, and that's why, by gawd, we're gonna have a full cemetery by tomorrow night. These four that died at the bank were just the start because they're bringin' in another three members of the posse that got shot dead."

"*Seven* of the town's men died?"

The old man spat again and his voice was bitter. "So, mister, you just showed me that you can count that high."

"I'm sorry," Longarm apologized. "I know this must be a terrible blow for Elk Creek, but I need to learn exactly what happened here."

"Why do you need to know, dammit?" the old man demanded. "You gonna go after them murderin' bank robbers and return all the hard-earned miner's gold and cash they stole from our town?"

"That's exactly what I intend to do," Longarm said.

The old man shook his head. "Are you loco or just light in the head? That gang will kill you just as quick as they killed the seven that will be buried in our new cemetery tomorrow."

"That may be true, old-timer, but I'm a United States Marshal and I have killed a lot of men in my own time."

The old man blinked with surprise and his eyes narrowed. "*You're* a federal marshal?"

"I am."

"Who the hell is the half-breed? Your reservation deputy?"

"He's my friend and, yeah, he's just become my deputy." Longarm looked sideways at Ira. "If you agree to be deputized, in addition to my sorrel gelding you'll be paid for your services, but it damn sure won't make you rich."

"I'll take the job, Marshal."

"Good."

The old man was taking all of this in and getting angrier by the moment. "You got a badge to show, mister?"

Longarm found it in his pocket and showed it to the old man, who walked up to his horse and studied it for a moment before saying, "Looks like the real thing."

"It is the real thing."

"But you're going to hire that dark-skinned fella on that pinto to be your *half-breed* deputy?"

"That's right, and I've got a posse that will be riding into Elk Creek in an hour or two."

The old man's eyes filled with hope. "How many men comin' in your posse?"

"Four."

He shook his white-crowned head with disappointment, then looked up at Longarm and said, "Well, four added to you two fellas makes six. That ain't enough, but it could work out, I suppose, if they're all damned good with guns and rifles. You fellas had better be ready to shoot to kill, because the gang that came through this town is fast and accurate, and every one of them is a cold-blooded killer."

"The four coming along to help me and Ira are all women," Longarm told the old geezer, figuring he might as well get out the rest of the story. "They were former slave women kept as captives at a trading post on the Navajo Reservation."

"*Slave women!* Jaysus, Marshal, have you been chewin' peyote or somethin' even worse! You can't be serious, and I don't think this is a damned bit funny!"

"Old-timer, these women are hard and they can all ride and shoot," Ira said. "Even more important, they are filled with hatred for the very men that just murdered seven of your town's citizens."

"They're *women*, you half-breed, half-brained nitwit!" the old man screeched.

Longarm could see that the old man was losing control of himself and might even have a heart stoppage, so Longarm tipped his hat, touched heels to his horse and rode on up the street saying, "Thanks for your time, old fella."

"I don't believe that you two are anything but *loco*!" the old man bellowed. "And this town ain't in no damn mood for any more crazies right now. Tell that story to anyone else and they'll shoot you dead!"

Ira trotted up beside Longarm and said in a low voice. "You really tipped the old man over the edge."

"I didn't mean to," Longarm gravely replied. "Let's ask that man sweeping the boardwalk in front of that saloon over there to tell us the rest of this story. Hey, mister! You got a minute?"

"Sure," the fat little man in a bowler, white shirt and string tie said, glancing at them as he kept sweeping. "What do you want?"

"I understand that a gang of masked men robbed your bank and emptied out all of its gold and cash."

"That's right. And they killed seven of our bravest citizens. Four here in town during the holdup and three more that went racing off with a half-assed posse bent hell-for-leather."

"And got themselves killed for their trouble."

"That's right. The posse was a collection of prospectors, townspeople and whoever else could find a horse and a gun real fast. Hell, some of them just had clubs . . . the poor, dumb bastards."

"So what happened?" Longarm asked.

"What happened is that they were only about fifteen minutes behind the holdup gang when they all went barreling out of Elk Creek. They didn't ride two miles before they charged into a massacre. The gang was hiding in some rocks just waiting for them to come, and when they opened fire . . . it was awful. We got shot-up people and three dead posse members. One of them was even the town's preacher."

"So the posse rode right into an ambush."

"That's right. And when the smoke cleared, what was left of the posse was runnin' for their lives back here to town."

Longarm shook his head. "And this happened when?"

"Two days ago about five o'clock in the afternoon, just as the mine shifts got off and the workers were coming into town to drink and eat."

"Any idea how much gold and cash the gang got away with?"

"Nobody knows for certain, and we probably never will have an exact amount of the loss. The banker, who kept all of the money and the records, is dead, but people are saying that the gang probably got away with at least ten thousand dollars' worth of gold and cash."

Longarm whistled. "That's a pretty big haul."

"They were a well organized bunch, and they were devils! They shot and gunned down good, hard-working men when they could have just ordered them to drop their guns and surrender. I know that they'll all fry in hell after they die, but for right now they're alive, and that's part of the hell that this mining town is living."

Longarm nodded. "Thanks for your time and information."

"You're welcome. The funeral service for all seven of those brave men will be held at the north end of town at our new cemetery tomorrow morning. Our only man of the cloth is among the dead, but we have a few Holy Bibles, and words will be read and friends will speak in remembrance. You're welcome to attend . . . You too," the man said, looking at Ira. "God doesn't show favoritism or care about skin color when he embraces the souls of the departed. Those good souls that come unto him will *all* find eternal salvation."

"Amen," Longarm said, tipping his hat in reverence. "But we didn't come to bury the dead. We came here to find, kill and bury the guilty."

The man stared up at Longarm and then at Ira. "You're going after that gang?"

"Yep."

"In that case," the man said, removing his bowler and mopping his damp forehead, "I had better tell our mortician to have two more caskets made and ready for a second burial service."

Longarm forced a tight smile. "Tell your mortician to have ready another nine caskets. And you can also tell your mortician to bill the federal government."

The man started to speak, but Longarm and Ira rode on down the main street of Elk Creek, taking in the town's sorrow.

"Where are we going now?" Ira asked.

"We're going to find the dead gang member that was shot to death."

"Why?"

"Because when the women arrive, I'm sure they'll be able to identify his body."

"And we don't already know it was Fergus Horn and his gang?" Ira asked.

"We know. But I just want to have it on the record before the showdown," Longarm said tightly.

Ira nodded with understanding.

Chapter 16

The dead gang member was laid out behind the mortician's office on a dirty old horse blanket. Flies were exploring and buzzing around the man's blood-caked body, and from the looks of the man's battered face, some of the townspeople had lost control and kicked the hell out of the corpse.

Ira took one glance and looked away quickly.

"Have you ever seen him before?" Longarm asked.

Ira nodded. "I saw him a couple of times in Holbrook. He was riding with Horn, but I don't know his name."

"The mortician is awful busy inside preparing the bodies of the townspeople that were shot. I wonder if he even checked this man's pockets,"

Ira shrugged.

"I'll check his pockets just in case there is any identification," Longarm said, fighting off the smell of decaying flesh.

A quick search revealed no papers of any kind, which was not all that surprising.

"What do you want to do now?" Ira asked, having walked off some distance.

"I think that I'd like to know if anyone recognized a woman among the gang. I'd sure like to know if Veronica was with them when they hit this town."

"If they wore masks and the woman is as thin as we've been told, I doubt that anyone here would even have realized there was a woman among them," Ira reasoned.

"You're probably right," Longarm said. "But at any rate, we need to wait for the women to catch up."

"Do we?" Ira asked, raising an eyebrow in question.

Longarm understood what this man was saying, and he'd given considerable thought to the idea of just outdistancing the former slave women. But the more he'd been around them since leaving Horn's trading post, the more he was beginning to understand that those women meant business and that they were not wilting flowers who would quit or run away in fright when the bullets started to fly. Rather, they were angry and filled with a need to exact a terrible revenge on Fergus Horn and his men.

"We need them," Longarm said. "And I promised they would be in on the showdown."

"What are we going to do here until they arrive?"

"Grain our horses, clean our weapons and take a nap. Sounds like a plan to me," Longarm said.

Ira smiled. "Yeah, that does sound good."

The former slave women came riding in about four hours later, and when they saw Ira's pinto and Longarm's sor-

rel in a livery corral, they hurried right on over to wake
the two men who were taking a nap in the barn.

"You shouldn't have left us!" Josie said, her voice
quavering with anger. "How come you rode off and left
us?"

"We needed to get here ahead of you women and ask
some questions," Longarm said by way of what he knew
sounded like a pretty lame explanation. "And I just figured that you'd be coming along not very far behind."

"What questions?" Rosa demanded.

Longarm explained what he and Ira had been up to
since arriving in Elk Creek. He ended by saying, "Ira
recognized the one dead bank robber that was laid out
behind the mortician's office building. I got a feeling that
the thief's body was pretty badly abused by the angry
crowd of townspeople. My guess is that the man won't
even rate a pine coffin. He'll probably just be thrown in
a shallow hole and covered up without any words read
over him."

"What did he look like?" Juanita demanded.

Longarm described the dead bank robber and all of
the women said his name was George Ballard, and that
the world was a whole lot better off without him. "Ballard was a pig," Josie spat. "I'm glad that he's dead."

"You women get some food at the café down the
street and rest up for an hour or two, and then we need
to take up Horn's trail," Longarm told them. "And, if any
of you are ready to quit for whatever reason, I'll understand. In fact, it might be the smartest thing you could
ever do for yourselves."

The four women exchanged glances, and when Teresa

spit in the dust, it was clear that they had reached a mutual and unspoken agreement to see this hunt out to the very end.

"All right then," Longarm told them as he consulted his railroad pocket watch. "In two hours we leave."

"What about saddles?" Rosa asked. "We could sure travel a lot faster with saddles on those Indian ponies."

"Yeah, you're both riding saddles, so we should, too," Juanita said.

"I'll see if I can find four saddles," Longarm promised. "They won't be new or much to look at, but they'll sure be more comfortable to sit on than the sharp backbone of a pony."

"I'll miss the feeling," Josie said, grinning.

Longarm was confused. "What . . . ?"

Suddenly he understood what the "feeling" was for these women whose pubic area rested on a bareback pony's withers. Longarm had heard that this could be very pleasurable for women . . . and now he blushed as he realized this was actually true.

"Your choice, Josie. Bareback or in a saddle. Either way you're going to have to ride hard and fast if we intend to overtake Horn and his gang of bank robbers."

"I want a saddle," she told him. "I can get you to do the other thing when we make camp tonight."

The women cackled with ribald laughter, and that sent Longarm and Ira headed out the barn door.

Chapter 17

The citizens of Elk Creek soon learned that a federal marshal from Denver was in their midst, and at first they were jubilant and ready to sign up with him and go "kill all them thievin', murderin' sonsabitches." But when they learned that the federal lawman had taken on a half-breed as his deputy, they were angry and baffled. And a short time later, when they discovered that Longarm was taking four tough-looking women along with him to either kill or arrest the gang that had robbed their bank, the citizens of Elk Creek became outraged.

"Marshal Long, are you completely out of your mind!" a man yelled as they rode up Elk Creek's main street. "What kind of idiot are you?"

Longarm rode side by side with Ira. He knew that an angry and disbelieving crowd was following him and the trading post women, and perhaps he should have reined in his horse and tried to explain. However, the more that he'd heard from the citizens, the more he realized that there was nothing he could say or do that would soothe their outrage and grief except to bring Fergus Horn and his gang to justice.

"You're gonna all be shot to shit!" a woman shouted from the front of a saloon. "You and those stupid women are going to be killed the minute that the gang sees you! You'd better hope you never find that bunch or you'll be feeding the vultures!"

"I'd say that these people don't have much faith in us," Josie said to Longarm as she trotted up to join Longarm and Ira. "They think we are all crazy."

"Let them think whatever they want," Longarm replied as they neared the end of the street. "But when we come back with the dead bank robbers, we'll suddenly be heroes."

"And exactly what are our chances of doing that?" Josie asked.

"Slim to none if we don't catch Fergus Horn and his gang by surprise and then shoot first and fast."

"I can damn sure do that," Josie assured him. "How about you, Ira? Are you as dangerous as you look?"

Ira ignored Josie, and soon they were out of town. The insults and taunts fell away and they began trotting along at a steady and ground-covering pace. Longarm had bought cheap used saddles for all the women, and they were making far better time than before. They still had two Indian ponies in reserve, but they were all thin and Longarm knew they wouldn't be able to outrun Horn's pursuit if the fight went bad and they had to retreat.

As if reading his mind, Ira said, "Those ponies aren't going to hold up for a long hunt."

"I know that," Longarm said. "And as thin and small as they are, they probably couldn't outrun a cow. But they're all that we have and the women aren't giving them up, so we'll do the best that we can."

"Then we'll just have to catch the gang and take them by surprise," Ira figured out loud.

"That's the way I've seen it from the start," Longarm told him.

"Here's where Horn and his men ambushed the posse," Ira said, galloping up a little ways and dismounting to study the ground. "You can see where the bodies fell, and those dark stains in the dirt are blood."

Longarm also dismounted and surveyed his surroundings. It was a narrow defile in the rocks, and he could tell at a glance that Fergus Horn had set up his men for a perfect ambush.

"Ira," Longarm said, remounting his sorrel, "the wonder of it is that any of the posse lived to get out of this trap alive."

Ira nodded his head in agreement. The women caught up and looked around the area, knowing what they were seeing and not asking any questions.

Longarm turned to them and said, "Horn and his bunch are seasoned killers and expert shots. What happened here was like shooting fish in a barrel. If we have any chance at all of coming out on top of Horn and his men, we're going to have to set a trap just as deadly as the one that we're looking at right now."

"We'll follow your lead, Marshal," Juanita said. "We figure that this is your business and you've done this before."

"I have," Longarm admitted. "But there are always

things that can and do go wrong. The important thing is that none of us panic or lose our nerve when the bullets and blood starts to fly. Gunfights are won or lost mainly on who is steadiest under fire, and I'm counting on every one of you women to stand your ground."

"We're not cowards, and we've also seen death," Rosa told him. "The men we're chasing abused us in every way possible, and we want them to pay for that. So don't worry, Marshal, we won't run if the fighting turns against us and we get shot up."

"Glad to hear that," Longarm said. "Horn and his bunch have already pretty much wiped out a posse, so they won't be expecting any more pursuit. That's to our advantage and I mean to make the most of it."

"Any idea of where they're going?" Josie asked. "Because unless I've lost my bearings, they're not headed straight back to Horn's trading post."

"I know," Longarm answered. "If I were to venture a guess, I'd say that they're heading southwest, back onto the reservation but not toward the trading post. I'm thinking that Fergus Horn has a gold mine that he's working somewhere up ahead."

"Can we have some of that gold if we kill them all?" Rosa asked. "God knows that we have that much coming after what they've done to us."

"You can have some gold," Longarm said. "But let's just focus on winning the fight we're riding into. Otherwise, gold means nothing if we die. Now, let's ride!"

All through the rest of that day and the next they followed the gang's tracks. Late on the third day after leaving Elk Creek, Ira pointed ahead, calling, "Look!"

Longarm squinted into the afternoon sun, trying to see what Ira was excited about. He'd already figured out that the half-breed had exceptionally keen eyesight and could see things that were invisible to the rest of them. "Is it Horn and his men?"

"No. It's some Navajo women and children."

Ira pushed his horse into a gallop and Longarm followed suit. The women whipped their thin ponies into a trot.

Ira rode up to a band of old women and children who were weeping and wailing in sorrow. He spoke to the old women in their language and they kept pointing to the southwest and shaking their bony fists.

"What happened?" Longarm asked.

Ira scowled. "These people were traveling to a healing ceremony when Horn and his gunmen chanced upon them. They only had a few old black-powder pistols and rifles, and it quickly became obvious that if they offered resistance, the white men would shoot them all dead. So they threw down their weapons and surrendered to the gang."

A very old Navajo woman was crying and talking fast, and she kept pointing her finger to the southwest.

"Did Horn and his gang take some of them away?" Longarm asked.

"Yes. This woman says that the white men took three of their men as slaves. She says they put nooses around their necks and dragged them off." Ira dismounted and walked off in the direction that the woman was pointing. He moved around in the brush and then stopped, bent down and studied tracks for a moment before returning to Longarm and the women.

"I can see the tracks of the hostages. They're heading exactly toward where the woman is pointing."

"Ask her if she recognized the leader," Longarm said.

A moment later, Ira translated. "She says that the leader was the man who owns the trading post off to the west. She also says that his wife was among the ones that fell upon them but that her hands were tied to her saddle horn."

"How long ago did this happen?"

"About noon today," Ira said after getting his answer. "She tells me that there is a gold mine out there about half a day's ride from here and that is where the whites are taking their men. She says that the hostages will be forced to work in a big cave and dig for gold, and that this is not the first time her people have been captured and then forced into the mine. She says that they never come back to The People."

Longarm considered this information in grim silence a moment before he said, "Tell her that the men that were taken today will come back alive. Tell her that we will bring them back to this place tomorrow."

When Ira told this to the old women, their faces lit up with smiles and then the smiles faded and there was more talk.

"What now?" Longarm asked.

"They want to know if the soldiers are close to help you."

Longarm looked at the old woman and shook his head. "No soldiers."

The woman spoke rapidly, waving her hands in the air.

"She wants to know where the other white men are to help us."

"Tell her that these four women are all good shots and

brave fighters," Longarm replied. "Tell them that these women were once slaves like their men who were taken today, and that they will fight to the death."

Ira slowly translated this message and the Navajo women and children stared at Josie, Juanita, Rosa and Teresa with a mixture of awe and disbelief.

Longarm's eyes lifted in the direction Fergus Horn and his gang were headed, and then he looked back at the old woman whose face bore the pain of much hardship and suffering. "Ask her and the others to offer prayers that we are victorious."

Ira nodded and translated. The Navajo women and children all bowed their heads and began to chant and pray, several making the sign of the cross. Their behavior reminded Longarm that Catholic priests and missionaries had been making converts in this harsh and unforgiving country for a very long time.

"Let's ride," Longarm said. "I'd like to sneak up on the gang and be in place tomorrow at sunrise."

Chapter 18

Longarm and Ira pushed their horses as hard as they could without leaving the women far behind. They tried to stay off the horizon where they would not be seen by Fergus Horn, although Longarm seriously doubted that the outlaws had any real concern about being followed.

Near dusk Ira rode alone toward the crest of a hill and dismounted. He dropped his reins and crept up to take a good look at the country toward which the outlaw band was headed. Longarm saw the half-breed crouch and then drop to his belly and lay flat for several minutes before he backed up, then stood and trotted over to rejoin them and the horses.

"The gold mine and the holdup gang are only about a quarter of a mile away," he announced to everyone.

"Then I'd better take a look," Longarm said. "In fact, all of you women ought to come up and take a look so you know the lay of the land and what we're up against."

Juanita said, "I'll stay and hold the horses. You can describe it all to me when you come back."

Longarm nodded with approval and the women dismounted. Their legs were stiff and raw from the long miles, and they walked bowlegged and awkwardly up the hill to then drop and inch their way to the top.

"My gawd," Josie said, shielding her eyes from the setting sun. "That's quite a mining operation!"

"Ira," Longarm asked, "how many men do you count?"

"Twelve or thirteen whites and the Horn woman. That's her sitting on a rock over by the cave's entrance."

"Yes," Longarm said, wishing he had field glasses. "I see her now. Veronica looks as thin as a boy."

"What are we going to do?" Rosa said, voicing the question that they all were asking in their minds.

"I'm thinking on it right now," Longarm replied as he studied the scene.

What he saw was a rock shack, a big set of corrals that contained all the gang's horses along with what appeared to be a few burros. About fifty feet from the mine's entrance was a pile of rock tailings as big as a house, then another small wooden shed that probably held dynamite and work tools. The mouth of the mine was at least twelve feet in diameter and was dug into the side of a sixty-foot-tall cliff. On top of that cliff was a broken mesa, and just off to the south in a shallow arroyo was a big stand of cottonwood trees that told Longarm this was the gang's source of precious spring water.

Other than that, there wasn't a lot else to be seen. It was clear that the men working in and around the mine slept and ate outdoors, and most of them were loafing in the shade of the rock house.

"The Navajo captives are probably already working in the mine," Ira said. "How do we handle this?"

Longarm licked his parched lips and looked at Ira and then the slave women. "We have to catch them with their pants down because there is no way that many gunmen are going to surrender. Given that sobering fact, we have no choice but to each select a man-target and open fire at the same time. There are six of us, and if even only three of us kill our targets, then we've evened the odds considerably."

"I'm not sure that we can get close enough to open fire on them before dark," Josie said.

"I'm sure that we can't," Longarm told her. "We'll make a dry camp and hit them with everything we've got right at dawn. We'll be on the east side of them, firing away from the rising sun, and it will be shining directly in their eyes."

"I could sneak in and open that corral then stampede off their horses and those mules," Ira suggested. "That way, if everything goes wrong, we'll still have our horses and we can move back out of their firing range."

"Good idea," Longarm told him. "Where do you suggest we make a camp tonight that is as close as we can get without being seen or heard by Horn and his gunmen?"

Ira pointed to the cottonwood trees. "If we go there and wait through the night we'll be in a great firing position come daybreak."

"I agree," Longarm said. "And, if necessary, we'll have the water and a place to make a stand."

"That's right."

And so it was decided. Longarm led his small but determined force down from the hill and they remounted their horses. He explained their sketchy plan to the women.

"We'll move into that big stand of cottonwoods after dark when we know that nobody will be coming there to fetch water. Just before first light we'll creep in closer to the camp and select our targets, making certain no one aims at the same person."

"I want to be the one that puts a bullet in Fergus Horn," Josie said, her voice low and hard.

"He'll be difficult to distinguish from the others in the poor early morning light," Longarm warned.

"I could pick him out among a hundred damned men."

"All right. He's yours, but shoot for the chest and try not to miss."

"I'll get him!" Josie swore.

Two hours after sunset they quietly entered the stand of cottonwoods. Their horses drank their fill and then were tied securely and kept saddled.

"I'll take the first watch," Longarm told them.

"I'll take it with you," Josie offered.

Longarm grabbed a blanket to sit upon while he watched the camp until midnight. The gang had built a huge bonfire and it lit up the otherwise dark skies with embers drifting toward the moon. The gang members were still celebrating their bank holdup and there was a lot of drinking, howling and coarse laughter. Near the mouth of the cave and huddled among themselves sat five or six captive Navajo mine workers. Their heads were bowed on their chests and they looked as if they were asleep or maybe just exhausted.

Longarm spread a blanket down and Josie spread another. "How far away are they?" she asked.

"Three hundred yards is all. Maybe a little more."

"I can almost smell their sweat across the sage," she told him. "Or maybe the smell is coming from us."

"We're pretty rank," Longarm said, "and I'll sure look forward to having a hot bath."

"A hot bath," Josie said with a sigh. "I can't even remember the last time that I had one. I guess it was in Holbrook last winter. Horn didn't ever let us take a real bath."

"Last winter? That's a long time."

"Well, I do wash regularly," she told him. "But I make do with a washrag and a pail of cold water. That's not the same as climbing into a steaming tub of hot water with real soap."

"No," Longarm agreed, "it sure as hell isn't."

Josie and Longarm sat side by side on their blankets, watching the bonfire and listening to the gunmen shout and raise hell. Off a little to one side of the fire stood a big man and a slight figure; Longarm was certain he was looking at Fergus Horn and his former wife, Veronica Sutton.

Almost as if she read his mind, Josie asked, "Did you ever know that lady back in Denver?"

"No. Veronica Sutton was way above my class and social standing. Her father was the governor of Colorado. Miss Veronica was Governor Charles Sutton's only daughter. She was a child of wealth and privilege. Veronica divorced Fergus Horn, and shortly afterward her father died after falling off his horse and breaking his neck. A day later the judge who signed the divorce decree died with a fish bone lodged in his throat . . . and he never ate fish."

Josie shook her head. "I'd bet anything that Horn killed both men and made it look like accidents just to get even."

"I'm sure that he did, but there were never any witnesses or evidence to the fact. Not long after that, Veronica just disappeared and people thought she might have run off to Europe or somewhere far away in order to deal with her grief."

"But she came here."

"Yes. Horn must have kidnapped and then taken her way up in Monument Valley where no one would ever think to look for the daughter of a deceased governor."

"How did that lady ever come to fall so far and end up with someone like Fergus Horn?"

"That's a question only she could answer, and I doubt that she knows herself after all the hell that she has been through. I expect," Longarm continued, "that she initially saw Fergus Horn as a dashing federal marshal and fell in love with the man, never suspecting that he had a dark side to him. I worked briefly with Horn when he was a federal marshal and he was a very handsome and charming man."

"Love really is blind," Josie said. "I've fallen for more handsome but bad men than I could shake a stick at. When it comes to men, I'm a terrible judge. It's gotten me into trouble all my life."

"It's gotten almost all of us into trouble a time or two," Longarm told her. "I don't know what it is, but sometimes a person walks into your life and you just completely lose your senses. Your brain stops working and other parts of your body take over your mind."

Josie dug a gentle elbow into his ribs. "And it happens to men as well as women?"

"Of course."

"Are you in love with that girl back in Denver?"

"You mean Molly?"

"Yeah. That's what you called her. You said that she was waiting for you to come back when you were finished here in Arizona. Do you love her and intend to marry her?"

Longarm frowned at Josie. "You sure are askin' a lot of personal questions."

She brushed his lips with her fingertips. "We just might get killed in the morning, so why not talk about what is important? Do you love Molly?"

He thought about it for a moment. "The truth is I like her a lot but I don't know if I actually *love* her. I'm not even sure what love is anymore, Josie, other than a crazy state of mind. And I don't even know if I ever want to experience that craziness again."

"But you have."

"Oh yes," he admitted. "But as I've gotten older I like to think that I've also gotten a bit wiser."

"If you can't love anymore, you've lost something pretty special in this life."

"I'm sure that's true. Have you been in love before?"

"*Dozens* of times, starting when I was about ten years old and skinny as an old broomstick."

Longarm grinned.

"Why, Custis, I'm in love with you right now."

"No, you're not! You don't even know me, Josie."

"Maybe not, but I know we made love and it was very special. Want to do it again?"

"Right here and now?"

"Why not?" Josie kissed his mouth. "Like I said before, we might die in the morning and I think that we ought to suck all the pleasure out of life while we still can."

Longarm glanced up just in time to see a shooting star. He took it as a good omen and then he put his arms around Josie and said, "You're right. Let's do it."

In minutes, they were undressed and locked together under the moon and stars on a dirty Navajo blanket, making love as if it were the last time they'd ever have the chance. Longarm felt Josie's short but shapely legs lock around his waist as she pulled him in deep her body and he thrust at her with pure, unleashed pleasure. Josie matched his thrusting with her own and when they finally reached their climax together, they each slapped hands over the others mouths to keep their all-important silence.

"Holy cow!" Longarm panted, lying on his back when it was all over and fighting for breath. "That was really special!"

"Yes," Josie said. "Are you in love with me now?"

"Maybe I am," he replied, kissing her lips. "But all I know for sure is that what we just did for each other was as good as it gets."

"We could do it again. We don't have to wake up our sentry replacements *exactly* at midnight, do we?"

He stifled a laugh. "No, we don't," he told her. "Nor should we."

And so, temporarily satiated by their lovemaking and very happy, they lay on their bare backs and gazed up at the starry heavens, holding hands like they were true childhood sweethearts.

Chapter 19

Ira touched a sleeping Longarm with the toe of his moccasin. "Marshal," he whispered, "dawn is less than an hour away and I'm going to see if I can stampede their livestock out of that big pole corral."

Longarm sat up and rubbed his eyes with the palms of his hands. "All right."

Ira glanced at Josie lying nearby. "I'd guess that you didn't get a lot of sleep last night."

"I got enough," Longarm told the half-breed. "How long do you think it will take you to sneak over to their corral and open the gate?"

"About a half hour. And when I do, I'll try to ease those horses out and drive them off to the west real quiet."

"We'll hold our fire until you're finished," Longarm said. "And be damned careful, Ira. Don't open fire until we do from this side, and watch out because you'll be in front of us and I don't want you to get shot by mistake."

"I'll stay low, and when some of them break for the

corral and the horses, I'll try to take down a few on my own."

"I'm sure you will," Longarm said, extending his hand. "Thanks for all your help. I couldn't have found these outlaws and this mine without you."

"I doubt that's true," Ira said a moment before he disappeared into the blackness of predawn. Longarm pulled on his boots and walked over to Juanita and Rosa, who had volunteered to take the last watch before morning. "Any activity?"

"A couple of 'em got up, staggered over to the tailings pile and took a piss, but then they went back to their bedrolls and sleep."

Longarm glanced to the east. "The sun will be peeking over those hills pretty soon. I'm going to wake the other women up and we'll move forward so that we can get in as close as possible before we open fire."

"Do you really think we'll survive?" Rosa asked.

"I do or we wouldn't be here," Longarm told her. "Just keep steady and hold your fire until I fire first. Then aim and don't rush your shots. The sun will be behind our backs and directly into their faces. That alone will give us a big advantage."

"What about the white woman and the Navajo captives?"

"All we can do is hope that they either duck or run for cover," Longarm told her. "But we can't hesitate. Fergus Horn's men are seasoned gunfighters and they won't scatter in panic like a lot of men would do under the same circumstances. No, those that survive our first volley will dig in and fight like hell."

The women nodded with understanding. Juanita

grabbed Longarm's sleeve and whispered, "I have a sister living in Santa Fe whose name is Margarita Lopez. Her husband's name is Jose and they own a cantina in the middle of town. If I die, will you . . ."

"You're going to be all right," he promised.

"You can't say that for certain, Marshal. None of us knows for sure that we will be alive one hour from now. So, if I don't make it, will you please give this to her and tell her that I died bravely?"

Juanita handed Longarm a silver and turquoise necklace. He cupped it in his hand for a moment and then slipped it into his vest pocket. "I'll do that," he vowed. "But you're going to survive this. Just stay low and keep shooting. If the bullets start getting close, roll to the side and don't quit firing. And whatever you do, don't stand up and try to run."

"We won't run," Rosa told him. "Those men have done bad things to all of us, and now it is our turn to get even."

"That's the spirit!" Longarm went over to his bedroll and picked up the eight gauge double-barreled shotgun. He loaded the monstrous weapon and knew that, even if he was out of range and couldn't hit any of the gang, the blast alone would damn sure scare them nearly shitless.

With the heavy old shotgun balanced in his right hand and his Colt .44-40 holstered on his left hip, he figured he was ready for battle. "All right," he hissed just as the sun crested the eastern horizon, "let's move in and take up firing positions!"

It was almost too easy as they crept toward the mining camp in the strengthening light. When they were in firing range, Longarm held up his hand and motioned the

women to spread out and take cover. His eyes strained
toward the pole corral and he finally saw a silhouetted
figure moving among the corralled livestock. A moment
later he heard the faint sound of quick hoofbeats as Ira
drove the outlaw's horses out into the open range.

"It's time," he said to Josie, who was crouched close
beside him.

Longarm raised the cumbersome shotgun, cocked back
its twin hammers and slowly squeezed one of the triggers.

The blast was incredible! Longarm saw flames shoot
out of one barrel, and the recoil punched him so hard he
staggered. Taking aim again, he fired the second barrel
off with similar thundering effect. Barrels smoking, Longarm reloaded the awesome weapon and raced toward the
camp. When he saw Horn's gunmen jumping up from their
blankets, he opened fire again with both barrels blazing.

An outlaw was swept off the ground and hurled backward as if a giant invisible hand had plucked him into
the sky. Longarm dropped the shotgun, dove behind some
brush and pulled his six-gun as the slave women opened
fire.

Gunsmoke and chaos reigned supreme and the outlaws that had not been killed in the opening salvo scattered like desert quail, taking their own firing positions.

Longarm almost shot Ira by mistake. An outlaw tried
to make a break for the mine and Longarm fired two
quick shots. One of them took the legs out from under
the man, and when he struck the ground he began crawl-
ing toward the mine opening.

"Jackson, you dirty bastard!" Josie screeched, standing up and firing at the wounded man who scrabbled
even faster across the hard, rocky ground. Finally, Josie

shot the man in the back of his head, blowing his brains across the rocks just as he was about to disappear into the mine.

Ira was crouched behind the tool shed and then he was running toward the defenseless Navajo captives who huddled in terror. Longarm saw the half-breed dive in among the captives with a knife in his hand to cut their bonds. Moments later, the Navajo hostages were racing for the nearest cover, which was back to the tool shed. Ira caught a wounded Navajo and carried him the last few feet to the shack and then slammed the flimsy wooden door behind him.

For a moment there was a lull in the fighting, and Longarm shouted, "Fergus, this is Marshal Custis Long from Denver! Surrender or all of you will be killed!"

"Go to hell!" Horn shouted from behind the tailings pile. "I'd rather die than hang!"

"You're pinned down and you can't escape!"

"We'll see about that!" Horn yelled back.

The firing resumed and the battle continued for nearly an hour. The last of the outlaw gang was dug in now, and Longarm figured there were at least four of them along with Horn

Josie was sobbing and holding Rosa, who had taken a bullet through the forehead and had died instantly. Another bullet had kicked up right in Juanita's face and the spray of dirt and sand had blinded her.

"Hang on," Longarm pleaded.

"My gawd, my eyes! I can't see!"

"Maybe it will pass. Just stay down and . . . and try to keep still. This thing is almost finished."

"Custis!"

It was Fergus Horn calling his name.

"Yeah?"

"Your hero took those Navajo into our tool and supply shed, and guess what's boxed in there with them!"

Dynamite!

"Custis, you surrender or we'll blow your hero friend and those Navajo all to hell! Do it now!"

Teresa and Josie glanced sideways at Longarm. "What is he talking about?" Josie asked.

"There's dynamite in that shed where Ira and the Navajo took cover," Longarm explained. "Ira wouldn't have thought of that since he's probably never worked at a mine, but now he's trapped. If he tries to make a run for it across that open space, they'll shoot him down. If he stays and we don't do as Horn says, they will turn all their fire on the shack and almost certainly hit the dynamite. Either way, unless we do what Horn says, Ira and the Navajo hostages are dead men."

Josie was stretched out behind a clump of brush. Now she dipped her head and pounded the dirt in frustration and anger. "We *can't* surrender. If we do that, Horn will kill us all for sure!"

"We're not going to surrender," Longarm said. "But I don't want to see Ira and those poor Navajo blown to smithereens."

"Then, what . . . ?"

"I'm *thinking*!" Longarm snapped. "How many men are still firing back at us?"

"Just three . . . well, maybe four."

"And one of them is Fergus Horn," Longarm said, thinking out loud. "And then there is the question of his former wife, Veronica Sutton."

"Maybe we shot her by mistake," Teresa offered. "When the fight started the light was so poor we couldn't have told her apart from the others."

"I know that," Longarm said, mind working furiously.

"Custis! We can make a deal here! I've got gold and cash. Lots of it from Elk Creek and from this mine. But we need to work a deal."

"No deals!"

"Then you can kiss those Indians goodbye and I'll bet you won't put in your report that you were also the reason that Veronica died today!"

"You're running a bluff, Fergus. I don't believe she is dead."

"She *was* hit and is wounded," Horn insisted. "Veronica is bleeding and I'll let her bleed out if you don't come out with your hands in the air, and you can tell my gawdamn trading post whores to do the same!"

Longarm swore in helpless frustration. What the hell could he do? If he refused, Ira and the Navajo captives would be blown to hell and Fergus was fully capable of executing Veronica.

But if he and the women threw down their guns and surrendered . . . Horn would not only kill them, but they'd be tortured.

"I won't go down there," Josie said. "I won't be under his control ever again. You don't know him, Marshal. He'll tie us up and do things to us that you can't even imagine before we die."

"I can imagine," Longarm grated. "But it's either us right now or Ira and the Navajo will die."

"Then they'll have to die because, if you surrender, all of us are as good as dead."

Longarm swore in frustration because, deep down in his guts, he knew that Josie was right.

Suddenly, Fergus Horn stood, dragging a feebly struggling Veronica Sutton along as his shield. He backed toward the mine entrance, and when he was standing just inside and out of sight, he shouted. "You saw her, Custis. The former beautiful 'Queen of Denver' is *still* alive."

Longarm had only caught a glimpse of Veronica, but he had seen her move and he knew that she really was alive. He'd also seen a lot of blood on her dirty dress, and the way she'd struggled told him that she was weak and helpless.

"Let her go and come out of there," Longarm shouted. "Fergus, it's over and you're finished!"

"The hell I am! Come and get me!"

Longarm drew a deep breath. He knew that if he stood up, the surviving members of Horn's gang would instantly cut him down in a hail of bullets.

Josie grabbed his arm. "No!" she pleaded. "He's just using her as *bait*. Don't do this."

"I can't just sit here and let her bleed to death," Longarm railed. "I just can't do nothing except let her die."

"She's going to die anyway."

"Maybe so, but I'm going to do everything I can to stop it from happening," Longarm said, reloading and checking his gun. "Just do your best to cover me."

Hearing this and knowing that she could not stop him from being killed, Josie bowed her head and began to cry.

Chapter 20

Neither Ira nor the Navajo captives that were huddled on the floor of the work shack could read, so the word *dynamite* stamped on the wooden box meant nothing until Ira overheard Fergus Horn's shouted death threat. Now, he was staring at the wooden box and realizing with a shock that *this* was Horn's hole card. Very carefully, Ira reached into the box and pulled out one of the sticks of dynamite and held it up for the others to see.

One of the newly captured Navajo cried out and recoiled in terror.

Ira understood at once that he had to somehow get rid of the dynamite. There being no other immediate solution at hand, he simply shoved the door open and hurled the stick toward the hired gunmen. The dynamite bounced harmlessly on the ground, telling Ira that it would not explode all that easily.

But it will explode if it is shot.

That's what Fergus Horn had used as his ultimate

threat, and Ira was sure that the threat was real. Speaking rapidly in the Navajo tongue, he told the others that they had to get rid of the dynamite and they needed to do it fast.

There were at least a dozen sticks in the box and Ira began snatching them, kicking open the door and hurling them with all his might toward Horn and his men.

"Shoot those sticks!" Josie cried, taking aim at one and missing badly.

"No!" Longarm shouted. "If you hit one and it goes off, it could kill Veronica!"

Fergus Horn had an entirely different set of instructions to shout to his remaining hired gunmen. "Next time that sonofabitch opens the door, fill it full of lead and kill him!"

Ira heard the man's order but he knew that he had to get rid of all the dynamite, so he kicked open the door and hurled another stick at the gunmen. Instantly, a fusillade of bullets knocked Ira to the floor.

"The door!" he yelled, knowing he'd been hit several times. "Close that door and everyone stay down!"

They somehow got the door shut without anyone else getting shot. Ira crawled backward, sliding in his own blood until he was leaning heavily against another Navajo.

"How many more sticks?" he asked, gritting his teeth against the pain of a bullet in his side. "How many more sticks of dynamite are in the box? Count them."

"Seven."

Ira knew that it would be suicide to try and hurl that many sticks out the door toward Horn and his gunmen. "There are work tools in here . . . picks and shovels. Find a weak or loose board along the back wall and bust it out! Do it fast," he grunted.

The Navajo grabbed tools and attacked the wall; it didn't take them fifteen seconds to locate a thin board and break it apart. Light streamed into the shack and Ira saw that he was losing a lot of blood.

"Knock out more boards so that you can run away. Hurry!"

The captive Navajo threw themselves at the wall using picks and shovels to bust through the wood and make their frantic escape. Ira watched them run through the brush and then race over a low hill. They were hunters, and inside of ten minutes Ira knew that the Navajo men would be impossible to find.

"Marshal! Don't surrender!" Ira shouted as he grabbed his Winchester and crawled out through the ragged hole in the wall. "I'm safe!"

Longarm heard Ira, and he'd seen the Navajo captives bounding over the hill to freedom. He grinned and had no doubt that Ira would soon follow them to safety.

"What do we do now?" Teresa asked, anxiously looking back and forth between Longarm and Josie. "Horn still has a couple of men left and if we . . ."

Suddenly, Longarm saw Ira's head pop up in the brush and the half-breed began rapidly firing his rifle at the work shack.

"He's trying to blow everything up!" Longarm yelled.

No sooner had Longarm cried those words than one of Ira's bullets pierced the wooden box holding the seven remaining sticks of dynamite.

The explosion was so thunderous and devastating that the work shack vanished along with the rock house, the corrals and half the nearby mountain of mine tailings. An immense cloud of thick, roiling dust rolled across the yard. Longarm ducked his head as flying rocks, shattered boards and all manner of debris filled the air and the sky high above.

"Oh my gawd!" Josie moaned, reaching out to grab Longarm. "We're all going to die!"

Longarm shouted at Josie to keep her head down, but his words were drowned in the roar that filled their ears and the choking dust that blanketed everything from sight.

Seconds passed while objects fell like meteorites from the boiling dust cloud overhead. Minutes passed and finally the dust cloud began to dissipate enough for Longarm and the surviving slave women to be able to see the devastation.

"No man could have survived down there," Teresa finally said. "Every one of them is dead."

"All except one Fergus Horn and the woman who made it into the mine. He still has his last card to play," Longarm replied.

And then, Fergus Horn shouted out from the mine through the cloud of vanishing dust. "You've got thirty seconds to come out with your hands in the air, Custis. Thirty seconds before I shoot Veronica."

"Would he really do that?" Longarm asked, knowing the answer.

"He would," Josie said without hesitation. "But he'll do it anyway after he kills you."

Longarm made a cruel decision. Cupping his hands around his mouth, he shouted, "Go ahead and kill her, Fergus! The minute that I hear the death shot we'll all open fire into the cave. Does it have a dogleg or is it straight? Bullets ricochet and we've got enough to make sure you never walk out of that mine alive!"

He heard Fergus Horn curse in anger. "All right! It's you and me now, Marshal. Come on, gawdamn it! Let's see who lives this morning and who else dies!"

Longarm stood up and knocked the dust from his clothes, and then he wiped his gun clean and blew his nose so that he could breathe freely.

Josie stood up and threw her arms around his waist. "You're going in there!"

"Yes."

"But he's the last one left alive. If we just don't let him come out then thirst will drive him out in a day . . . maybe two . . . and then we can shoot him down like a rabid dog."

"But in the meantime the woman from Denver, who never hurt anyone, would die," Longarm explained. "Josie, I'm her only chance. Go see if you can help Ira. Go along now, girl."

Josie started to plead, but when she looked into Longarm's solemn eyes, she knew that nothing in the world that she could do or say would change his mind.

Chapter 21

"Here!" Josie said as he was starting to walk toward the mine. "Take this shotgun into that mine with you and blow Fergus Horn straight to hell!"

She had picked up the forgotten but massive eight-gauge, double-barreled shotgun and was now insistently shoving it at Longarm. "Do you have any more shells?"

"As a matter of fact, I have exactly two left."

"Two is enough. Kill him!"

"Go help Ira. If Fergus Horn walks out of that mine instead of me, then you're going to have to kill him or he'll kill you, Ira and the other trading post women."

"I know that."

Longarm took the shotgun and loaded it with the last two of the six shells he'd bought from Horn's friend, Dan Shelby, seemingly a hundred years ago.

He checked the pistol on his left hip and marched through the thinning cloud of dust, amazed at the total devastation caused by the blast of dynamite. He had no idea how many sticks had caused such destruction, but it must have been plenty.

There weren't even any recognizable human remains in the mining yard. Just small pieces of clothing and smears of blood and splinters of bone, some protruding from shattered boards. No one to bury. Nothing to claim or find.

When Longarm stopped at the mouth of the mine he cocked back both hammers of the shotgun and stepped just inside, crouching low.

How deep was this cave? How far back did it run and was it a straight run to the end . . . or did it curve?

Longarm remained in a squat while his eyes tried to adjust. He couldn't see a damn thing ahead, but then, after he was ten feet into the mine, neither could Fergus Horn.

"I hear you!" Horn shouted, his voice a hollow sound. "Come on, big man! I'm waiting and Veronica is dying."

"You miserable sonofabitch," Longarm grated, moving from one side of the mine to the other. "You murdered Governor Sutton and that Denver judge that signed your divorce papers and made them both look like they died accidentally."

"Yeah, I did!" Horn barked a laugh. "And I was pretty damned good, wasn't I."

"Yeah, but you didn't get away with it."

"Oh yes, I did. The question I have is why did they finally send you out to Monument Valley after me?"

"Veronica managed to get a bloody note off the reservation asking for help. Someone passed it on to Billy Vail, and he sent me to arrest or kill you and then bring the former governor's daughter back to Colorado."

"Well, well! How neat and tidy an explanation. I wonder who passed the note? Veronica was always writing them. I don't know how many I intercepted and they were pretty pathetic. I used to read them to her aloud and bring her to tears."

"Why did you keep her hostage after your divorce?"

"She is still my wife!" Horn shouted. "I love her and she's my wife no matter what they said or did back in Denver."

"Yeah, she was your wife at first. But then she learned what kind of a monster you really are and forced you into a divorce. Fergus, you should have accepted that and moved on. You had the looks and brains to do something important."

"I moved on, all right. I built a trading post, and there is gold in this mine. Maybe not the fortune I thought it was six months ago, but still enough to give us all the wine and women we'll ever need."

"You have gold fever, Fergus, and it's addled your mind," Longarm replied, crouched low and tiptoeing forward, determined to keep the man talking. Judging from the sound of Horn's voice, the killer was now only about fifty feet ahead.

Keep him talking.

"If you're reasonable, we could work out a deal," Horn suggested. "I would be willing to give you all the gold and cash from that bank holdup we pulled off in Elk Creek. It amounts to over ten thousand dollars. And I've got a lot more gold right here at the mine."

"Maybe it was all blown to dust in the explosion," Longarm suggested. "Did you keep it hidden or locked away in the rock house? If so, the rock house isn't standing anymore. In fact, the rock house doesn't even exist."

There was a long silence and desperation was creeping into Horn's voice. "We could recover it, Custis! Maybe not all of it, but most, and that would still add up to a fortune. And we could capture more Navajo slaves to work this mine until the vein runs out. That was my plan all along. I needed to stir these Navajo people up. A little uprising and then the cavalry would crush them and relocate them out of this country until this gold mine peters out. All mines peter out eventually, but who knows how much gold is left?"

"No deal," Longarm said flatly. "Just surrender and you live."

"Live to hang? Not very damned likely!"

Horn unleashed two blind shots and both of them ricocheted harmlessly off the rock walls and out into open air. Longarm dropped to one knee and raised the big shotgun. He had seen Horn's muzzle flashes and knew exactly where to aim. At this range, he figured he would blow Horn's head completely off the man's shoulders.

But then he heard Veronica moan and his finger froze. *Where is she? On the ground. He wouldn't have her in his arms because then he couldn't really shoot very well.*

"What do you *really* want, Custis? Are you attracted to my wife? Is that what is making you so unreasonable? I recall that you were at our wedding, and wasn't it a grand affair? All those dignitaries. The French champagne flowing like water and the flowers and beautiful people. Everyone congratulating me and Veronica and telling us what a lovely couple we made together. Yet all the time they were lying through their teeth because I'm a half-breed!"

Horn's laughter was ragged, chilling and ugly. "You don't think I know what you and the rest of the people at that wedding were saying behind our backs? How you all couldn't imagine why a beautiful white girl with a wealthy and powerful father could be so stupid as to marry a poor, half-breed lawman like me?"

"Some were saying that, I suppose. But you really did make a handsome couple. And you could have raised yourself to a higher level instead of ruining everything you'd been blessed with at the time."

"Bullshit! Veronica . . . well, I learned that Veronica never *really* loved me."

"Then why did she marry so far beneath her station in life if it wasn't for love?"

"I have a big cock," Horn snickered.

"I don't believe that."

"Just as I don't believe that what really drove you all the way out to Arizona and this reservation isn't that you fell in love with my wife and now you want to rescue her like some knight on a white horse. I know she inherited everything from her father and you also want her Denver money."

"Money isn't all that important to me, and as for the white horse . . . well, I'm riding a sorrel," Longarm said, inching forward. "And I'm asking you one last time to throw down your gun and come out of this mine alive."

In reply, Fergus Horn cursed and fired again, this time his bullet coming much closer. Longarm saw the muzzle flash and made an instant mental calculation.

The gun flash will be about waist high. Aim the shotgun much higher so that its blast will go over Veronica lying on the floor.

With a quick prayer that he was judging it right, Longarm threw the shotgun to his shoulder and pulled both triggers. The shotgun belched flame and the noise was so deafening that it made Longarm stone deaf.

He rushed forward, stumbled over a soft body and dropped beside it. Brushing his hands over the body, he knew it was Veronica Sutton. He blindly scooped her up in his arms and staggered backward until he fell across the entrance of the cave with dazzling sunlight in his eyes and a roaring in his ears.

Teresa cried out and ran toward them. Josie came running, too. Longarm was dazed but unhurt. "Is she alive? Is Veronica still alive?" he kept asking. "And what about Ira and . . . and Juanita!"

Longarm, Ira and the slave women, along with Veronica Sutton, stopped for two days to rest and heal at Ira's hogan. His wife fed them, Navajo medicine men came and did their ceremonies and healing while Ira's happy children lifted their spirits with laughter and simple games.

Ira would have a full recovery and so would the former governor's daughter.

"When we get to Holbrook," Josie asked as they sat alone together outside the hogan watching a magnificent sunset, "are you and that lady going directly back to Denver on the train?"

"Yes, we are."

"Will you fall in love with her like you fell in love with me out in Monument Valley?"

"I'm afraid that I might." Longarm shrugged. "I don't know. Haven't we both admitted we're just a couple of fools when it comes to love?"

She took his hand and held it tight. "I admitted it. You didn't."

He knew what Josie wanted, and it was a gift he was glad to give. "I loved you, Josie. I loved you."

"You mean that?"

"Yes." He kissed her mouth. "But we've got a long ride tomorrow. It's time to go to bed."

"Together," she insisted. "We've still got a couple of nights together, and you did say that you loved me."

"All right," he told her. "Let's go to bed together for a couple more nights."

Josie lay her head against his broad shoulder. "That's enough to give me a fresh and good start," she murmured contentedly. "And a good new start is all I'm gonna need."

Longarm smiled because he knew that this was true.

Watch for

LONGARM AND THE KILLER COUNTESS

the 383rd novel in the exciting LONGARM
series from Jove

Coming in October!

And don't miss

LONGARM AND THE RAILROAD WAR

Longarm Giant Edition 2010

Available from Jove in October!

LONGARM

GIANT-SIZED ADVENTURE FROM
AVENGING ANGEL LONGARM.

BY TABOR EVANS

penguin.com/actionwesterns

M456AS0510